I0583734

BURNT OUT

OUT

Jan- A Henderson

Black Hart Entertainment

Edinburgh. Brisbane.

First published 2019 by Black Hart

Black Hart Entertainment.
Blackhartentertainment.com

The rights of the author to be identified as the author of this work
has been ascertained in accordance with the Copyrights, Designs
and Patents Act 1988.

Publisher's Note: This is a work of fiction. Names, characters,
places, and incidents are a product of the authors' imagination. Locales and public names are sometimes used for atmospheric
purposes. Any resemblance to actual people, living or dead, or to
businesses, companies, events, institutions, or locales is completely
coincidental.

Cover by Panagiotis Lampridis (BookDesignStars)
Book Layout © 2017 BookDesignTemplates.com

Burnt-Out.
ISBN 978-1-64570-607-6 (Print)
ISBN 978-1-64570-608-3 (eBook)

> *Burnt-Out. Noun.*
>
> *1. Totally destroyed by fire.*
>
> *2. Physically or emotionally exhausted.*

Thanks to Arthur

Dedicated to all the fire-fighters world wide who risk their lives to keep us safe.

Duncan Lawson got out his digital recorder and notebook.

The grey-haired woman sat at a plywood desk opposite him, quickly scanning the notes he had handed her. Duncan noticed the sleeve of her white medical coat was spattered with dried blood, while the far wall had a line of bullet holes running along its surface. Neither observation put him at ease.

Nor did the armed bodyguard, standing dispassionately a few feet away. His shaven head glistened under the harsh lights, illuminating every pucker of the lumpy scar running from one ear into his bushy beard. Duncan nodded politely and got a menacing frown in return.

"So you're Arthur Lawson's son," the woman said finally. "A newspaper reporter, no less."

She didn't sound particularly pleased.

"His stepson, Dr Banner." Duncan was in his twenties and visibly nervous. "He was a good dad, though."

3

"I still don't know why you want to talk to me. The story of Arthur and the Collingwood fire was fully covered a long time ago. I was only a teenager back then."

"I found your letters to my father," Duncan replied. "You were obviously close, yet he never once mentioned your name. Not even to me."

He shrugged.

"That seemed weird. Call it a newsman's instinct if you like."

"You've done a good job of digging out other old documents." Banner placed the papers on her desk and pushed them away. "But I don't know why you went to so much effort or what you hope to find. I never mentioned the blaze in anything I wrote to him."

"No. Dad wouldn't talk about the fire either. None of the people involved ever did. Don't you think that's odd? I do."

Duncan reached out and switched on his recorder.

"Will *you* talk about it?" he asked. "I think there's a puzzle to be solved and you're the missing piece."

Dr Banner hesitated.

"I suppose I'll have to," she sighed. "Partly because I want you to stop digging. Partly because you deserve to know the truth. However, it has to be off the record."

"I came a long way." Duncan couldn't hide his surprise. "You agreed to meet with me, after all."

"And here we both are. I'm sorry but those are my terms."

She sat back and waited.

"I convinced my editor to let me take time off for this trip," the reporter protested. "Promised I'd come back with *something*."

"You'll have to decide what's more important," Dr Banner replied casually. "Getting a news story or finding out what actually happened."

"But… I…"

The bodyguard tapped his weapon and raised a shaggy eyebrow, as if daring the man to object some more. His eyes were hard and cold.

"Do we need the heavy here?" Duncan licked dry lips. "He's freaking me out."

"That's his job. This is a dangerous area and my hospital has been attacked twice in the last few months."

Duncan gave up.

"All right." He reluctantly turned off the recorder. "Please continue."

Doctor Banner folded tanned hands on her lap. Then she began to recount the story of the Collingwood fire.

Not the famous version.

The real one.

Part 1

Arthur and Sargon

> *The thing about living with any disability is that you adapt; you do what works for you.*
>
> Stella Young

1

Its official name was Eden Heights but everyone called it the Eyesore.

Twenty-one stories high, perched on a windy hill overlooking the city, the towering building had once been Collingwood Infirmary. But that was back in the 1960s when tower blocks were all the rage and architects were hell bent on reaching the sky. By the time of the fire, age had discoloured its concrete facades and the high-rise had fallen into a state of disrepair. A replacement NHS Collingwood had been built next door, lower and glass fronted, with carefully tended lawns, modern equipment and a Starbucks.

Now Eden Heights was finally scheduled for demolition and most of the patients had been transferred to the new hospital. Few would miss the ugly grey finger, though even critics confessed the building was still handy. Doctors and nurses hid behind it when they went for a sneaky cigarette. Its massive bulk protected the surrounding area from blustery weather that constantly swept across the hilltop and it was a handy place to store supplies and spare apparatus.

It was useful for another reason. Though nobody would admit the fact, it had been the perfect place to house the least competent nurses and most 'difficult' patients.

The complainers. The weirdos. The troublemakers.

And a teenager called Arthur Lawson, who was considered to be all three.

2

The door to room ten slammed open and Sargon Danaan stomped in, leaning heavily on a crutch, an insolent sneer disfiguring his lips. The boy's lower leg was in a cast and he acted like he was ready for an ambush.

The door hit a rubber stop and bounced back, knocking the support from under his arm. With a yelp, Sargon pitched forward and landed face down on the bed.

"Stupid... walking stick." He spat through a mouthful of sheet. "I may snap it and throw it out the damned window."

He quickly pushed himself upright, wobbling slightly. Standing on one leg, he gingerly leaned backwards to scoop up the crutch, plaster cast held delicately out in front for balance. Teeth gritted, the boy inched lower, fingertips scrabbling at the handle.

He began to slowly tilt.

"Oh... Son of a bitch."

Sargon vanished backwards and hit the floor, sending up a puff of dust, injured foot sticking into the air like a piece of road kill. A string of thickly accented foreign curses filled the room and two spade like hands gripped the bedclothes as the boy began to pull himself up. His thick mop of black hair appeared, then a frown of epic proportions, welded over pupils, dark as wet stone.

The frown deepened as he properly took in the room. Two beds with threadbare covers. A cracked sink. Discoloured cream walls. Grubby windows reinforced with latticed wire.

And a teenager in a wheelchair, watching him.

Sargon gave a start.

The room's other occupant had cropped hair, pasty white skin and irises so pale they seemed almost translucent. Though slightly built, his shoulders and arms were muscular and his hands calloused. He didn't smile or say hello, making the atmosphere even more unfriendly.

"What in flaming hell are *you* staring at?" the burly intruder growled.

The stranger didn't avert his intense gaze and the covers Sargon gripped were slowly sliding off the bed. He sank down a few inches.

"Stop looking at me funny with those creepy peepers," he warned, slipping even lower. "You do not know how to blink?"

"I'm staring into space." The watery glare never wavered. "You just happen to be in the way."

Sargon finally scrabbled onto the bed and rolled over, breathing heavily.

"It is far too hot in here." He wiped sweat from his brow. "I am toasting like a hoarse chestnut."

"Yup. Welcome to hell."

"I was in anticipation at getting my own room, at least," Sargon continued grumpily. "How is it you have *your* own room?"

"I don't anymore," the boy replied. "You're in it."

"Hah! I am used to getting a cold welcome, even in this hothouse." Sargon waved his hand dismissively. "It is water off my duck's back and I do not care."

"That's all right," the boy shrugged. "I asked to have you brought here."

"I am not here because you wanted it, this I can tell you with no problem," Sargon grunted. "I am in this crappy dump because of my hitting a kid in one of the main wards."

"If you say so." The boy scratched his cheek absently. "How come you managed to hit him with a broken foot?"

"I did not hit him with my foot." Sargon looked puzzled. "That would be kicking him. I gave him an old one-two with my walking stick."

"Suppose that's like a punch and a kick combined. With a weapon thrown in."

"Yes indeed." Sargon seemed pleased by the observation. "I am likely inventing my own martial art."

"Why did you hit him?"

"I am not in a quiz show, nosey creature," Sargon warned. "Where I come from, it is best not to be too inquisitive."

"Where *are* you from?" The occupant didn't seem put off by his veiled threat.

"Ward 4."

"I mean, which country? You look kind of... Arabic."

"This is why I thumped the other kid. Always he was probing me with his inquisitive tongue."

"I'm pretty sure you didn't mean that the way it sounds."

"And he stole my banana." Sargon stretched and yawned. "So don't you be...."

"Look. I don't really care," the stranger interrupted. "Don't care where you're from either if the truth be known."

"Then why do you ask?"

"It's polite. You going to thump *me* for being sociable?"

"You do not seem very sociable to me."

"Says the guy who goes around whacking people with his crutch."

"You should be putting a sock in that smart upper lip." Sargon gritted his teeth. "It is good luck for you that I have standards and would not hit someone with glasses."

The boy looked surprised. It was the first expression to cross his face since the intruder arrived.

"I'm not *wearing* glasses."

"You are in a wheelchair," Sargon said. "Surely that is worse."

"Thanks for pointing out the obvious." The occupant gave a thin smile. "Wasn't sure you'd noticed."

"I am trying not to mention it."

The boy glared at his new roommate for a few seconds longer. Then he seemed to come to a decision.

"Name's Arthur Lawson." He stuck out his hand formally. "You must be Sargon Danaan."

"How do you come by that information?" Sargon recoiled from the gesture.

"I guessed." Arthur withdrew his hand. "It's a common enough name."

"Nothing about me is common." Sargon looked around and spotted a chart fastened to the bottom of his bed. "I am betting my details are on that. You have read at it before I came in."

"I'm confined to a wheelchair, Einstein." Arthur rolled his eyes. "My legs don't work."

"You steer a wheelchair using your arms," Sargon replied pointedly. "I fear I have been stuck with a nutty chap. What did I do to deserve that?"

"You thumped a kid in Ward 4 for starters," Arthur reminded him.

"It is hardly starting World War III."

"You're here 'cause I asked," the boy repeated. "I need help with a little task, but keep that on the quiet for now."

"Am I looking like your butler?" Sargon scowled. "Fetch a nurse."

"Don't want the staff knowing what I'm up to." Arthur tapped his nose secretively. "So I told them I'd like someone to talk with."

"They are not going to move anyone in here just because you asked."

"You're in my room, aren't you?" Arthur kept a poker face. "I may have thrown in a few words like lonely and depressed to make sure it happened."

"And you wanted *me*?"

"Actually, I told them I wasn't fussy." Arthur looked his new companion up and down. "They must have taken me at my word."

"Well, I am not here to do your bidding," Sargon snorted. "And I have no interest in our chins wagging."

"Good. I don't want to listen to you droning on in broken English. *I* don't mind talking, though. Nurses aren't great listeners and my invite to Beyoncé obviously got lost in the post."

"I would think double about talking." Sargon sat up and folded his arms. "Everything you say so far makes me want to punch your head."

"I'm used to getting a cold reception," Arthur replied snidely. "But you'll help me in the end."

"What makes you so certain of that?"

"Cause there's nothing else to do in here. You'll see."

"Do not be counting any chickens." Sargon settled back down on the bed. "I have been kept in far worse places than this."

"Like where?"

"Ward 4." Sargon closed his eyes. "Excellent try, however."

3

An hour passed. Sargon opened his eyes again and began counting the discoloured spots on the ceiling. After forty, he gave up.

"Do you have a mobile telephone? I must take a picture of this room and post it on Instagram. Tell my friends never to be getting sick."

"You have friends?" Arthur feigned astonishment. "You don't seem the type."

"I think you are a pot calling me black," Sargon shot back. "Do you have a mobile or not?"

"Nah. They took it away when I tried to have pizza delivered."

"And I have left mine behind by mistake." Sargon glanced up at an empty bracket high on the wall. "Where is your television? Even ward 4 had a television."

"I did have a TV at one time," Arthur admitted. "They took it away too after the remote got stuck on the sports channel."

"There is nothing wrong with sports. I am liking figure skating myself. Every athlete should wear sparkly costumes for cheerfulness."

"There's plenty wrong if you can only be a spectator."

"Indeed. I suppose you could not reach the button to turn it off."

"No," Arthur replied sourly. "I had to use the remote."

"But you were saying the remote was stuck."

"Yeah." Arthur mimed a throwing motion. "It got stuck in the TV screen."

Sargon raised an eyebrow.

"That's why I need your help," the teen continued. "As you can see, I have mobility issues." He gave a thin laugh. "According to the hospital psychologist, I have all sorts of issues."

"What are you thinking this is?" Sargon tapped his cast. "A fashion accomplice? If so, I should draw the polka dots on it." He sniffed disdainfully. "Though it is plaster of Paris, I do not feel very stylish."

"At least you can stand up."

"You cannot get out of the wheelchair at all?"

"Oh, sure. I'm just too lazy to walk around."

"What happened?" Sargon ignored the sarcasm.

"I don't really remember." The teen pointed to his head. "My doctor thinks I have post traumatic stress."

"Hah!" Sargon blew a raspberry. "I am not accepting that nonsense."

"Oh." Arthur's eyes widened. "Nonsense is it?"

"Everybody has hardships to bear in this life. They are to be overcome. What else is there to do?"

"Does it take everybody half an hour to go to the toilet?"

"Then you have enough problems," Sargon replied reasonably. "No need to be adding crazy to the list."

"I'll sure as hell go crazy if I keep listening to you." Arthur spun the wheelchair so he was facing away from his new roommate. His hand caught in the spokes and the boy yelped in pain.

"Like you say, I've enough problems as it is."

To emphasise the point, he stuck bruised fingers in his mouth, terminating the conversation.

Sargon looked at the hunched back for a while, then swung his legs carefully off the bed.

"I apologise," he said. "I am easily angered and was sure I would get my own accommodation. I do not like the crowdyness and crying in the big ward."

Arthur stayed silent.

"All I was conveying is that you cannot be wallowing in misery like a sad hippo. You must find a way around the things you cannot achieve." Sargon stroked his dimpled chin. "We cannot fly, for an example. So we invented parachutes."

"Sorry," Arthur revolved back, carefully this time. "Did you just compare me to a sad hippo?"

"I am still learning to speak English."

"When did you start? Last Tuesday?"

"That was not nice." It was Sargon's turn to look offended. "It is certainly a pity I cannot hit you."

"Just give it your best shot." Arthur raised his fists. "I'll soon show you who's wallowing."

To his surprise, Sargon grinned.

"That is better!" he nodded. "Already, there is an advantage you have with your crippledness. You can hit people and they will not be smacking you in return."

"You are unbelievable."

"I am a practical fellow, is all."

"Sounds more like you're scared." Arthur beckoned. "C'mon. Put em up. Overcome *that* hardship."

"I have learned my lesson in ward 4." Sargon's grin widened. "There will be no fisticuffs with a boy in a wheelchair, or I am likely being moved into the cupboard."

"What happened to not wanting to talk?" Arthur changed tack. "You've been yapping ever since you got here."

"I am feeling sorry for you," Sargon replied evenly. "That is what you desire, is it not?"

"Stop with the self-pitying jibes," Arthur snapped. "Want to see how I get round my handicap? By getting people to do exactly what I tell them."

"Hah!" Sargon laughed. "You do not live in the real world, I am thinking."

"No. I live in here."

The newcomer had no answer for that.

"Let me show you what I mean," Arthur continued. "Press that buzzer on the wall,"

"This one?" The boy picked up his crutch, clumped over to a red button and pushed it. "What does it do?"

"There." Arthur blew on his fingers. "Told you to press it and you did exactly what I said."

"Suddenly I am wondering if the cupboard is not such a bad idea." Sargon leaned his head wearily against the wall.

The door opened and hit his crutch, knocking it out of the boy's grasp. He took a few steps backwards, arms windmilling, before his injured foot gave way. Sargon landed flat on his back with a loud gasp.

"What's going on?" The door was forced further open, pushing him under the sink. A large nurse peered through the gap. Spotting the prone figure, she gave an exasperated groan.

"What on earth are you doing on the floor?"

"I am checking the plumbing." Sargon reached out a hand. "It is old and smelly. That will be £45."

The nurse hauled the boy to his feet and steered him to his bed.

"I've heard about your escapades in ward 4," she said sternly, plonking him on the covers. "Don't be trying any of your nonsense with me."

Turning to Arthur, she put both hands on broad hips.

"Hello again Mr Lawson." Her smile was strained. "What can I get you *this* time?"

"Hi Doreen." Arthur gave her a cheery wave. "Think I could have a glass of water?"

"*Another*?" The nurse glowered. "I'll go fetch one. But this is the last time."

She turned and strode out again.

4

"See?" Arthur did a little shoulder wiggle. "Does everything I tell her."

"She did not look very happy about it."

"I'm not surprised. That's the fifth glass I've asked for today."

"You do not like nurses?" Sargon sounded genuinely shocked.

"No," Arthur retorted. "I don't like bloody nurses. Or doctors. Or psychologists."

"In my country, those are like angels of mercy. You should be more respectful."

Arthur was about to reply when Doreen came back in, carrying a full pitcher.

"This should keep you topped up for a while." She placed it on the bedside table and pressed a hand against the boy's forehead. "How are you feeling?"

"Numb. And I hate my roomie." Arthur grumped. "Why isn't he an out-patient? All he's got is a leg in plaster and he can get around fine with a stick."

A guilty look drifted across Doreen's face.

"I'm... eh... sure I don't know." She quickly bent over and took Arthur's pulse. "I have rounds to make,

25

so please don't buzz again. Especially not the emergency button."

"Oh, I didn't press it," Arthur replied innocently. "The new kid did."

"Did he now?" Doreen fixed Sargon with a steely stare. "You've only just got here and already you're causing a ruckus?"

"He instructed me to push it," Sargon objected.

"You don't strike me as a young man who does what he's told."

"You have got me there." The boy raised his hand. "May I have a glass of water too? It was a long walk from the proper hospital where staff are kind."

"It's best you exercise that leg as much as possible," Doreen said frostily. "Kitchen's just down the corridor."

"And he could surely wheel there." Sargon pointed at Arthur. "Why don't you make him get his own water too?"

"Our friend refuses to leave his room." The nurse shot the wheelchair bound boy an exasperated look. "Believe me, we've tried to motivate him."

"Try not bringing any more water. That will motivate him plenty, I am thinking."

"I heard you were sent to the Eyesore because you're a disruptive influence." The nurse leaned close, face inches from Sargon's. "But I will not allow you to agitate Arthur. He's enough of a handful already."

"He's sitting right here listening, by the way." Arthur broke in.

"I am still learning your language," Sargon said. "Is handful another word for insane?"

"The child is in a wheelchair. Show some sympathy."

"He tried to get me to fight him."

"Oh really?" Doreen peered at the newcomer over the top of horn-rimmed glasses. "Do you think I'm an idiot?"

Behind her back, Arthur nodded vigorously and Sargon stifled a smile.

"Your antics aren't funny." She jabbed a fleshy finger into the boy's chest. "Cause any more hassle and I'll have you moved out in two shakes of a lamb's tail."

"There's a cupboard down the hall," Arthur suggested helpfully.

"That's enough from you too," Doreen said irritably.

"I do not wish to be a beast of burden." Sargon tugged at the neck of his jumper. "But could we have some fresh air, perhaps? I feel like I am back in the desert."

"I wish we could," Doreen sighed. "But a few years ago, some woman chucked a chair through the glass on the 15th floor and jumped." She twirled a finger round her temple. "This place used to be mainly for psychiatric patients, you see."

"That explains a lot." Sargon glanced at Arthur.

"So they put in windows that don't open, with small panes of reinforced glass you can't break." Doreen indicated the filthy rectangles. "They need specialised cleaning too, but that hasn't been done for a while. Not when the place is going to be empty soon."

"Can you not turn the heating down?"

"Same story." A wistful look crossed the woman's face. "The old janitor used to regulate the basement boilers - but he took early retirement when he found out Eden Heights was getting demolished. The new guy only comes over from the main hospital a couple of times a week and doesn't know his arse from his elbow."

She jabbed a thumb at the ceiling.

"The power has even cut out a few times. It only lasted a couple of minutes but it's a good job there are no operations conducted here anymore."

"Indeed. If I paid taxes, I would surely be asking for a reprobate."

"We'll all be moving out in a week or so." Doreen looked at her fob watch and frowned. "So, stop moaning, for God's sakes. You don't hear poor Arthur complaining."

"Actually, I complain all the time," Arthur corrected. "Nobody listens."

"Enough, both of you! Let me get on with my rounds."

She left without a backwards glance.

"Well done," Sargon said, once she was gone. "You have got the tubby nurse to hate me in less than five minutes."

"She doesn't like me either." Arthur seemed unperturbed. "She just can't show it. Another advantage of my... what did you call it? Crippledness."

"I have already apologised and will not say it twice." Sargon leaned over and poured himself a glass. "But, if the staff are at your becking and calling for everything, why do you need me?"

"Not quite everything." Arthur took a sip of his water.

"I want you to get me out of here."

5

Sargon looked warily at his new companion.

"The well-rounded sister seemed happy enough for you to go outside," he said. "Like her, I am confused as to why you will not leave this room. I shall be giving it zero stars on Tripping Adviser."

"I've no desire to be paraded around the hospital grounds for ten minutes like a freak." Arthur drained his glass. "I want you to take me to the roof."

"The roof?"

"It's a flat thing on top of the building. Stops the rain getting in."

"Then you had better find yourself another pushy person." Sargon shook his head. "If I am caught smuggling you up there, I will not be moved to the cupboard. I shall more likely be put in a dumpster bin."

"We'll go early evening. There's hardly any nursing staff on then and they're usually kipping in an empty room somewhere."

"There must be cleaners working too. Even if they are doing a terrible job."

"I'm depending on that," Arthur smiled slyly. "I got a finely timed plan all worked out. Just need you to come along for the first part."

"Not on your nelly, rude boy," Sargon repeated. "I am black enough in the hospital books, and I do not even like you."

"Thought you might say that." Arthur began to rock violently from side to side. "Sorry about this."

"What are you doing?" Sargon struggled from the bed and landed on his cast. He cried out in pain and sank to the ground. "Stop it!"

"When I tip over, the crash will bring Doreen back." Arthur rocked harder. "I'll say you did it. That's assault."

"You are being ridiculous in a most epic manner!"

"I'm finding a way round the things I can't do like you suggested." The wheelchair tilted alarmingly. "Once the police cart you off, I'll get a roommate with a bit more guts."

"It will be your word against mine."

"I'm white and disabled and you look like a jihadist. Who do you think they'll believe?"

"All right! I will help!" Sargon launched himself forwards and grabbed hold of one wheel. "But this is a low and dirty trick."

"I know." Arthur stopped moving. "And I really do apologise. But I got to get on that roof. And I have to do it tonight."

Sargon had to admit, he sounded genuinely contrite.

"It seems to me you are having all the time in the world." He rolled onto his back and glared up at the boy. "I do not think you have a bus to catch up there."

"Heard there's going to be a huge lightning storm tonight," Arthur explained. "I want to watch it."

"You have a window."

"Which is too grubby to see through. Anyway, my eyes only come up to the sill."

"You cannot ask your family to take you when they visit?"

"The roof is off limits." Arthur shook his head. "And I don't have any family."

"Ah," Sargon said softly. "This is true for me also."

"Let's not exchange sob stories, eh?" The boy looked quickly away. "I just need this one favour."

"Then I will take you with massive reluctance or be spending most of my afternoon on this dirty floor." Sargon used the wheelchair to pull himself into a sitting position. "Though how we will manage this journey with my injured foot is a kettle of fish we have not fried."

"We'll get there if we work together." Arthur reached out his hand. "And I'll be forever in your debt."

"Those are adult words and you have shown yourself a child." Sargon refused the offer of help. "Made an enemy when I might have been an ally."

"And you're a hypocrite." Arthur quickly withdrew his hand. "Think I haven't guessed why you really hit that kid?"

"I am already telling you," Sargon said. "He took the banana I was saving for midnight snacking."

"I bet you did it so you'd be put in a private room."

"You are talking out of your buttock cheeks." The teen shuffled back to his bed, unwilling to continue the discussion.

"Yeah? I saw how you came barging in, ready to intimidate me. Thought you'd scare me into asking to be moved." Arthur gave a smug smile. "Except I'm not scared. Not able to move much either."

"If you keep accusing me of falsities," Sargon sulked. "I shall be moving some teeth around that big mouth."

"Now who's being childish?" Arthur retorted. "At least you had company in ward 4."

"I have had *your* company for one morning. And you are already blackmailing me."

"Then get me to the roof. We won't get caught." Arthur tapped his watch. "The night staff don't make their rounds until eleven and you'll be back by then."

He leaned forward.

"In return, I'll ask to be transferred. Say you snore or smell or something. Deal?"

"I am supposed to be trusting you?" Sargon looked doubtful. "You are like a James Bond villain in that wheelchair. I should be getting you a pussy to stroke."

"That didn't come out right either," Arthur pursed his lips. "And I don't lie, by the way."

"You were going to tell the portly nurse I pushed over your wheelchair."

"That was more of an exaggeration," the teen back-tracked. "I wouldn't really have done it."

"Pah! An exaggeration is just a fib waving its arms around."

"That doesn't make any sense."

"*You* don't make any sense." Sargon stuck out his tongue.

"Look. Let's start over," Arthur groaned. "If you help me, I *will* be your friend. And you *will* get this room to yourself. I promise. I really promise."

Sargon pondered this.

"*Please.*"

"I, too, can be sneaky I will take you as far as the top floor but no further. Then I am leaving and will be coming straight back."

"You don't want to see the storm?" Arthur asked. "There's going to be lightning and everything. Might even hit the roof."

"I am overwhelmed by indifference," Sargon said dismissively. "For I have seen much worse destruction from the skies. You must make your own way down again."

"Suits me," Arthur seemed strangely pleased by this. "I'll manage somehow."

"Let us get some rest, in that case." Sargon lay back and put both hands behind his head. "I am cat of eye and hard of shoulder but my leg is aching and in need of recharging for this ordeal."

Arthur stayed where he was.

"Are you not going to lie down? Or will you be sitting there until you melt in this heat like an evil snowman."

The teen pulled off his jumper and tossed it in a corner. His T-shirt was soaked with sweat but he kept it on.

"If you intend to be watching me with those spooky eyeballs, I will most certainly not begin kipping."

"I'll lie down." Arthur wheeled over to his own bed. "But I'd appreciate it if you didn't watch."

"Oh, I am happy to not to be seeing you." Sargon pulled the pillow over his head. "I have only been here two hours and am already losing the will to live."

"Now you know how *I* feel."

"Indeed I do. I am rapidly going off in my trolley."

Sargon closed his eyes and listened to Arthur grunting as he manoeuvred himself out of the wheelchair and removed his clothes. It took a long time. Eventually, he heard the creak of bedsprings and a long sigh.

"Thanks, Sargon."

"Perhaps you are blessing me in disguise." The teen removed the pillow. "It is so boring here that I must do something exciting or I will wake up in a coma."

He gave a short laugh.

"Anyway, I am often being told that trouble is my middle name."

"Really? Mine is Winston."

"That is a stupid middle name."

"Not as stupid as Trouble." Arthur rolled over. "Wake me up at five. Five exactly."

"Excellent. Now I am your speaking clock as well."

"Not with that dumb accent." Arthur switched off his bedside lamp. "I still don't understand why you're so desperate to have your own room. Only the bottom four flours are occupied and we'll all be moved to the new hospital by the end of next week. You wasted your journey coming here."

"I have my reasons," Sargon whispered, too low for Arthur to hear. "But those, you certainly do not need to know."

Sargon listened until his roommate's breathing grew calm and rhythmic. In all honesty, he wasn't too worried about getting caught, for he had a knack for getting out of difficult situations. Besides, nobody had actually told him the roof was off limits, so he could use that as an excuse.

Sargon chuckled to himself.

Arthur thought he was being very clever, blackmailing him into doing his bidding. But he had played right into his new roommate's hands.

The truth was, he was perfectly happy to take the boy onto the roof.

For he had a secret plan of his own.

6

The patient arrived at our medical station on the 24th January, looking like a rock lobster and suffering from third-degree burns. I am guessing he is a survivor of the air strike which targeted Arbhanjar the day before. If so, he must have walked for many miles to reach us, despite his injuries, and is certainly a v. resilient fellow. In the boy's pocket was photographic ID, identifying him as Sargon Danaan, plus a document stating he was part of a refugee convoy - one that was hijacked in the area a few days ago.

I cannot begin to guess what horrors he witnessed or what he and the rest of the convoy suffered at the hands of their captors. I do not think I want to.

All I know is he refused to say a word.

39

Sargon was put in the burns ward, which was packed with injured and crying children. He was quick to show his displeasure at the situation by head-butting the orderly (who I never liked, as he constantly picks his nose) and was given his own tent. Indeed, he would lash out when anyone tried to examine him but did not smile, cry or show any other emotion. Nor did he speak the whole time he was there. Therefore I diagnosed him as having post traumatic stress disorder.

But there was something about this enigmatic chap I liked, so decided I would be making it my personal mission to help him.

I tried to coax Sargon out of his shell, but my efforts went down like a balloon of lead. That was until he saw the Oxford Dictionary I carry around, so that I may learn better English. I was happy to be lending it to him, as I am already an exceedingly fine wordsmith.

He read it several times, from cover to cover, then found an English handbook on Fire Safety and Evacuation Procedures (which I had never finished because it is boring). Nevertheless, he pored over it endlessly until he knew it by heart.

He was a very strange fellow and no mistaking.

After a month Sargon Danaan had learned enough phrases to speak in halting English, so I began to chat with him daily. He was obviously clever with his clogs, for he became fluent very quickly, until he was almost

as good as myself. (And I am rather an eloquent gen-
tleman, with an accent the ladies are very fond of).

Using my charm with the nurses, I managed to get
him an Encyclopaedia and some English comics, which
he was most delighted to possess. Fortunately, we were
both big fanatics of superheroes (especially the green
Hulk), so we read them aloud together. I also gave him
a notebook to write new words.

His violent behaviourisms gradually vanished and
he became kind, thoughtful and decent, even assisting
me on my rounds. He was especially good with trou-
bled patients, being large and strong and knowing how
to perform a superior choke hold.

Now he had learned English he could talk off a don-
key's leg, so I questioned him about the fate of the
refugee column. However, this was one subject on
which his lips remained tight and I am not sure he even
remembers it.

I am thinking young Mr Danaan's PTSD caused
him to reject everything he had known before, even his
own language. I think he wished to re-invent himself,
as it were. This is something I can sympathise with, as
I am married to a terrible woman with a moustache. I
yearn to be employed as a Gondolier in Venice, where
I will not be shot at.

I am a doctor, not a psychologist, as they say in Star
Trek (that is my little joke) but I will never know if my
efforts had any real effect on Sargon. For, one night,
he left the camp and was never seen again.

He did leave a note on his bed, thanking me for the comics.

Since I had taught him perfect English I assumed he would head for Britain, though how he would manage that hazardous journey was a different kettle of fish to fry. Yet he obviously did.

I was devastated to hear, after surviving so much, that he died in a fire there.

7

Sargon woke with a start, jolted into consciousness by the unmistakable feeling of a grip on his shoulder. Instinct kicked in. A meaty hand shot from under the covers and grasped his assailant by the neck.

"It's only me!" Arthur choked, his face turning an alarming shade of red. "Chill out, will you?"

"Apologies!" The teen quickly let go. "You must not touch me when I am sleeping like a log."

"Make that a ninja log." Arthur wheeled back a few feet. "I thought you were going to kill me."

"The day is not over yet." Sargon rubbed both eyes and inspected his roommate. "You are looking exceedingly presentable all of a sudden."

Arthur had on a fresh pair of jeans, a clean hooded top and his hair was neatly combed. Sargon wondered how long it had taken to make himself so smart.

"I was afraid you were going to oversleep," the boy reprimanded. "Me? I've been awake for an hour."

"I shall be ready in two shakes of a lamb's tail." Sargon tested the new phrase he had picked up from Doreen. "Then we will embark on our moronic enterprise. I am sure it…."

He did a double take.

"What in blue blazers are you doing with *that*?"

A silver vase was balanced on Arthur's lap.

"It's a funeral urn," he said. "You keep cremated people's ashes in it."

"I am familiar with the disturbing object," Sargon goggled. "Does it contain anyone you know?"

"Nope," Arthur grinned. "Found it at the back of a cupboard on the next floor a few days ago. I went and got it while you were napping."

"I thought you were a hermit crab who does not leave his room."

"So do the nurses," his companion replied deviously. "Which is just how I like it. I'm a bit of a wheelchair ninja myself."

"This is very cheeky," Sargon tutted. "It may be someone's mother."

"It was stuck behind some towels, Sargon." Arthur patted the receptacle. "So, obviously, nobody wants it. And I'm pretty sure the occupant is past caring."

His eyes narrowed.

"Why? You're not some fanatic or something, are you?"

"My skin is dark and my accent foreign, racist chap," Sargon replied testily. "This does not mean I am concealing a bomb inside my trousers."

"*There's* an image I won't be able to get out of my head."

"I am no longer even religious," the boy continued. "If there is a God, his ears shall surely be burning over the things I have said about him."

"Preaching to the converted, buddy." Arthur propelled himself to the door. "Now get yourself moving. My scheme requires precise timing."

"Why are we requiring a jar filled with pieces of corpse?" Sargon began pulling on his clothes.

"All part of the plan."

"If the plan involves throwing it at anyone who discovers us, I am not a happy rabbit."

"Just get ready."

Sargon cleaned his teeth and helped himself to another glass of water while Arthur fumed with impatience. Finally, the boy signalled he was ready.

"Here we go," Arthur whooped. "The Three Musketeers, ready for an adventure!"

"There are only two of us."

"You're forgetting about the guy in the urn."

A thought occurred to Sargon.

"What if chunky Doreen checks the room?" he said. "And we are not here?"

"How many euphemisms for fat do you know?" Arthur asked pointedly. "Despite that terrible accent, you're a one legged thesaurus."

"It is important for me to practise new words." Sargon pulled a notebook from his pocket. "I write them down in this, for there is much of your tongue twisty language I have still to learn."

"Yet you know the meaning of euphemism?"

"Of course," Sargon said confidently. "It is a kind of trumpet."

Arthur squinted at him suspiciously. He had the niggling feeling that Sargon's grasp of English was far better than he pretended - and that he was putting on the comic accent. But the boy was eager to get going and did not question his new ally further.

Sargon was scribbling furiously in his journal.

"Can't that wait?" Arthur scowled.

"Hold on to your high horse." Sargon tore out a page and handed it to his companion. "Read this."

Dear Nurse Doreen

Arthur feels much better now that he has someone his own age to talk to. So he has asked me to take him for a jaunt in the hospital grounds, in order that we may look at girls. He wishes to convey his sorrow at being such a poopy-head and not going out before.

Much love. Sargon Danaan.

PS. We will be back in an hour or so. Please clean the room.

"Poopy-head?" Arthur was taken aback. "What are you? Five?"

"This way everyone will think we are outside," Sargon shrugged off the insult. "And not be perturbed if they find us missing."

Arthur frowned again. 'Perturbed' seemed too so-phisticated a word for Sargon's limited skills. But he shrugged the doubt off, impatient to get going.

"That's clever, I suppose." He tossed the note onto his bed. "Now, can we leave for the damned roof?"

They opened the door and ventured nervously into the corridor.

There was nobody in sight. The Eyesore had so few patients left that only a skeleton staff was needed, and Arthur had timed their exit well. The nurses were on their break in the staff room below.

Getting around was easier than they anticipated. Sargon had abandoned his crutch, leaning on the wheelchair handles for support. Arthur wedged the urn between his legs and helped propel them by pushing the wheel rims.

"This is easy as peas," Sargon grinned. "I should be signing us up for the London Marathon race. I will be 007 and you can be Number 2."

"Sure." Arthur smiled back. "Right after I win gold at the Paralympics, eh?"

"I still do not know why you need me. You are man-aging to perambulate along without any difficulty, I am thinking."

"There you go again," Arthur said. "What person learning English says perambulate?"

"If I am to speak your language properly, I would like to know *all* the words," Sargon replied. "To do otherwise would be lazy, would it not?"

"You're smarter than you appear, buddy." For the first time, a trace of admiration crept into Arthur's voice.

"It is my curse." Sargon pushed his companion around a corner. "I am far too gorgeous to be thought intelligent, though I *am* exceedingly brainy. But the ladies do not seem to mind."

"Here we are," Arthur said excitedly. "Next stop, the roof."

In front of them was an elevator. Sargon hit the call button and, after a few minutes, the grey door slid open. He manoeuvred his charge inside, wincing at the pressure it put on his injured foot.

"Well?" Arthur tapped his thumbs together.

Suddenly, Sargon knew why the boy needed him.

He couldn't reach the higher buttons.

"I tried using a walking stick to press the top floor a few times," Arthur explained. "But the buttons on this lift are old and stiff, like everything else in the bloody place. I can't manage it."

"Allow me, Sir Duke of Earl." Sargon reached over his head and jabbed floor 20. "I am assuming you will be expecting a pipe and slippers warmed for your return."

"And a foot massage. Not that I'll be able to feel it."

The elevator rose, creaking and grinding, until the doors opened again. The teens emerged into another corridor lined with empty offices.

"This is where hospital management was based until a few days ago," Arthur whispered. "But their offices are being moved into New Collingwood, so the place is deserted."

"Why did they stay so long in this horrible building?" Sargon wheeled Arthur into a large room. The furniture was covered in dust sheets and reams of paper, photocopiers and filing cabinets were stacked in one corner. "The hospital next door has a café filled with western delicacies like Egg McMuffin, with little sachets of ketchup."

"Doreen says the top floors had a proper restaurant, off limits to patients and nurses," Arthur snorted. "I bet that's the real reason it took so long for the Eyesore to be condemned. The bosses didn't want to come down and mingle with the sick and lame."

There was a world of hurt in his voice.

"With people like me."

"Yes. It is easier to ignore suffering if you cannot see it," Sargon said quietly, spotting tears welling in his companion's eyes. "That is human nature."

He grasped the wheelchair handles and pulled Arthur back into the corridor.

"Let us get you to your destination."

8

Police Report on the Assault of
Farid Asfour at Niddrie Mains,
Edinburgh

On the 5th of May at 15.30, Lothian and Borders Police were called to a disturbance in Niddrie Mains. On arrival, they broke up an altercation which had resulted in several injuries.

The officers interviewed a local resident named Farid Asfour, who was wearing a nabiq headscarf. She claimed to have been surrounded by four youths, who began telling her to go back where she came from, using abusive and racist language. When she ignored them, they pushed and jostled her. The incident was witnessed by a passer-by, who identified himself to the police as Sargon Danaan.

According to Mrs Asfour, Danaan intervened and demanded that the assailants leave her alone. The group then physically attacked him.

Despite being younger than his adversaries, Sargon Danaan managed to incapacitate all four. One was knocked unconscious, one suffered a broken nose, one a broken jaw and arm and another a fractured skull. Sargon Danaan was also injured in the fight, breaking his foot while stamping on an attacker's head.

After the altercation was broken up by officers, Danaan was polite and offered no resistance. The constables, at first, expressed doubt that this youngster could have inflicted such injuries on a gang of known troublemakers. However, several witnesses confirmed the boy was the victim of an unprovoked assault and simply defending himself, so no charges were brought. Instead, he was escorted by the police to Collingwood Hospital.

The incident was treated as a hate crime.

Additional Note.

Lothian and Borders Police later confirmed that the home address given by Sargon Danaan was false. Though he claimed to be a resettled refugee, they could not find him in the official database. They informed hospital authorities that this information had been passed to the Immigration Department, who intended to question the boy further and ascertain his legal status in the country.

The fire in Eden Heights broke out before they had the chance and Sargon Danaan died in the conflagration.

9

The boys edged out into the hallway and continued to an alcove at one end. Inside was a short flight of stairs leading up to a closed door.

"Here we are," Arthur announced.

"This is indeed a foolish errand." Sargon halted. "Though I am incredible, like the green Hulk, I will never be getting you to the top."

"Next part of my cunning plan coming up." Arthur took a deep breath.

"Hello!" he shouted. "Can anyone help us?"

"I knew I could not trust you!" Sargon thumped the back of his companion's head. "This is the very opposite of us not getting caught."

"Have a little faith," Arthur replied calmly. "Hello! Is anyone there?"

A large man, wearing grey overalls and holding a mop, emerged from one of the rooms. He strode towards them, wiping his hands on a cloth.

"What the hell are you doing on this floor?" he scolded. "It's not for patients."

"Nurse Doreen was taking us to the roof," Arthur held out the urn. "We were going to scatter my father's ashes."

"On top of the *hospital*?"

"He was a… eh… janitor here until he retired," Arthur lied, remembering what Doreen had told them. "Then he died of a heart attack. He loved the place, so it seemed appropriate."

"Oh. Sorry kid." The cleaner looked around. "Where's this nurse, then?"

"She had an emergency call. Told us she'd be back in an hour, but it will be getting dark by then and there's a storm coming."

"You'll just have to wait until tomorrow, I'm afraid. It's already pretty windy up there."

"But today was dad's birthday," Arthur said forlornly. "This was his last request. I *promised*."

"I'd love to help you," the man grimaced. "It's against the rules, though. And my shift is finishing, so I couldn't bring you back down."

He looked at his watch.

"The wife's picking me up soon We're off to the airport for a week in Majorca."

He glanced at the urn uncomfortably.

"First holiday we've had in two years. After that, I'm getting moved to the new buildings."

"I will get you up there, my friend, never fear," Sargon broke in. He sat on the stairs and inched up a couple of steps. He grasped the wheelchair handles and pulled until veins stood out on his neck.

"Harder, Sargon," Arthur urged. "We can't let pops down."

"What if nobody comes and you're stuck up there?" the cleaner asked uncertainly.

"Big Doreen knows where we are going and told us to ask anyone we saw for assistance." Sargon's face was turning scarlet. "She will be here soon, I am certain."

He tugged again and winced in pain.

"I will keep trying, Arthur. I shall succeed if it takes me all night."

"OK, OK." The man dropped his mop. "Let me have a go or you'll do yourself a mischief. Name's Tommy, by the way, if you want to mention how helpful I've been."

He grabbed the wheelchair back and began to bump Arthur up the stairs. The boy winked at Sargon, who was struggling along behind, using the rail for balance.

The trio reached the landing and Tommy opened the door. They emerged from a square concrete structure. As Arthur rolled onto the flat roof, the man helped Sargon up the last few steps, picked up a brick and jammed it under the door.

"There's a barrier round the perimeter, but don't go near it anyway," he cautioned. "And don't move the brick. If the door closes, it locks automatically and I'm the last of the domestic staff on until tomorrow."

"Doreen gave us her key," Arthur reassured him with another fib. "Thank you so much for helping, though."

"No problem, wee guy." The man awkwardly shook hands with Arthur. "My condolences on your loss."

Sargon was looking across the vista, mouth open. The clouds had briefly parted and a sinking sun was bathing the Pentland Hills in a lambent glow. In the distance, far below, the rooftops and gothic spires of Edinburgh sparkled like tiny, luminous pearls.

"Spectacular, isn't it?"

"It is pleasing in the extreme," Sargon breathed. "I am feeling like Allah, looking out from heaven for something to smite."

"Would you mind escorting my friend Sargon back down the stairs?" Arthur said. "He was just chumming me."

"No. I am fine." Sargon took in a lungful of fresh air. "It is most peaceful up here and I am in need of cooling down after manhandling you."

"I don't think that came out quite right," Tommy said.

"And I'd quite like to be alone with dad." Arthur patted the urn in agitation. "Just me and him."

"I shall keep a respectful distance, never fear." Sargon stretched and let the strong breeze blow over his body. "Considering this great windiness, the ash you are scattering will be ending up all over the place."

"Well, if you must." Arthur looked strangely put out.

"The foreign guy is right. It's best if you're not on your own up here." Tommy patted his arm. "I've really got to go. Take care now."

He turned and trotted back down the stairs.

"Aren't you going to leave me here?" Arthur asked petulantly. "That's what you said before."

"I shall depart presently." Sargon looked at his watch. "I still have a couple of hours."

"A couple of hours until what?" Arthur rounded on his companion. "I thought you were afraid of getting caught."

"You told the cleaner my name, smarty pants. I am surely busted anyway."

"Guy's off on his holidays with his missus." Arthur pointed out. "He'll have forgotten all about us by the time they come back."

"Then I am sorry for doubting you," Sargon admitted. "Your plan was a fine one."

"And you followed my lead perfectly," Arthur replied grudgingly. "You're as good at lying as I am."

Sargon's lips tightened and an awkward look flitted across his face.

Tommy got in the lift and took it to the ground floor, then walked down the stairs to the basement car port, where his wife was waiting. But he didn't like leaving those boys on the roof unsupervised and figured he had better tell someone about it.

As he emerged into the dimly lit parking bay, he spotted a female figure gliding along the wall.

"Hi there," Tommy said loudly. "Sorry to disturb you."

The woman whirled in surprise. Her face was obscured by shadows but there was no mistaking the nurse's uniform she was wearing.

"Just wanted to let you know there are a couple of kids on the roof," Tommy said, glancing around for his wife's vehicle. "Both got mobility issues, so I thought I'd better inform someone. One of them is up there scattering his father's ashes."

"Ashes?" The nurse sounded alarmed.

"Yeah. He's got an urn." Tommy spotted his wife's car and gave her a little wave. "Coming honey!"

"Ah." The nurse nodded slowly, face still hidden. "I'll check it out."

"Appreciate that." The cleaner said. "Have to go, though. Holiday beckons and the missus can't wait to see me in my new Speedos."

The figure waited until Tommy had climbed into the car and driven off. Then she raced for the stairs.

10

I was finishing my shift, cleaning the top floors when I saw two boys carrying an urn. They said they had permission to scatter their father's ashes on the roof. They said they were with a nurse who had gone to some emergency and would be back soon. I forget her name but they told me she said it was OK.

So I let them onto the roof, but I had to leave as my shift had finished. I was going on holiday and it was my first proper break in years.

I did tell another nurse about the kids, I swear. She was in the basement car park and promised she'd go sort it out, so I took her at her word. Why wouldn't I?

My wife was waiting for me so we drove straight to the airport. I didn't know about the fire until we landed in Majorca, a few hours later and I saw it on my Twitter feed. I phoned the authorities in Britain as soon as I heard, but the building had been destroyed by then.

When I got back, the police told me the boys weren't supposed to be up there and no staff had reported they were on the roof. But I wouldn't just leave them without telling anyone. I let that nurse know, honestly.

It ruined my holiday. I've done nothing but think about it since

Now I'm signed off on sick leave for stress.

11

Arthur and Sargon properly took in their surroundings. At this height, the gale was truly fierce and seemed to be coming from all directions, whipping the teens' hair around their heads.

One half of the roof was littered with scaffolding. The other was covered in a giant tarpaulin, tied at each corner, lifting slightly and rattling ominously with every icy blast. A smattering of plastic skylight covers, slumbering translucent turtles, allowed a weak glow to emanate up from the strip lighting in the offices below. Near the edge was a large wooden tower on steel supports.

"This is not quite what I was expecting." Sargon sounded disappointed. "What is going on up here?

"My guess is they're removing anything valuable before they demolish the building," Arthur said. "Copper pipes and any fitments that can be sold off. They'll start on the roof and work their way down."

"It is blessedly cool." Sargon glanced up. "But also blowy enough to send a jumbo jet off course."

"If you're not going to leave," Arthur said. "Why don't you find a chair and watch the storm with me. The workmen are bound to have a couple stashed somewhere for their tea breaks. We can sit under that big tank for cover."

"Good idea." Sargon plodded off. He stopped and looked over his shoulder. "Shall I fetch you one?"

"Don't sweat it," Arthur replied wryly. "Got my own."

"What a foolish thing for me to say!" Sargon winced. "I shall go exploring before I cause myself further humiliations."

Arthur waited impatiently until his cohort had vanished around the concrete block, then pulled a pair of leather gloves from one pocket and pulled them on. From the other pocket came a small sports camera with a rubber strap. He pressed record and slipped the strap over his head so the device was pointing out, like a miner's lamp.

Sargon had reached the far end of the roof. Finding nothing to sit on, he was on his hands and knees, peering under the rattling tarpaulin.

Arthur began to wheel himself through jagged pieces of scaffolding, heading in the opposite direction. His arms pumped faster and faster as the wheelchair gathered speed.

"I cannot find anything comfortable for my nether regions." Sargon backed out from under the awning. "Perhaps the workmen have…"

His eyes widened.

Arthur was almost at the other end of the roof, back hunched and head down.

"What in the name of Allah are you doing?" Sargon made after his companion. "Come back here, imprudent rascal!"

The boy only wheeled faster. Without his crutch, Sargon was reduced to a staccato hobble with no chance of catching up.

"I am back to not trusting you!" he shouted, limping behind the boy as fast as his injury would allow. "Arthur! I am begging you. Stop!"

The gale whipped away his words.

Arthur reached the roof edge, ringed by a low wall about four feet high. He slammed his wheelchair into the barrier and grabbed hold of the top. Carried forward by momentum, he hauled himself up and half way over.

"Do not do this!" Sargon bellowed. "I no longer want your stupid room!"

Arthur was draped across the wall like a discarded towel, upper body hanging over the edge of the parapet, useless legs still dangling on the roof side.

"Dammit!" he cursed, looking down.

The wall wasn't at the edge of the building, after all. Instead, there was a drop of ten feet onto another ledge, ending in an iron railing. The boy couldn't even see the ground.

"No!" he wailed. "This isn't fair!"

He hesitated, then grasped hold of one knee and tried to pull it up.

"C'mon you wimp," he muttered to himself. "Just swing round and drop. It's not like you can hurt your legs any worse. You won't even feel it."

He got one knee on top of the wall and reached for the other.

Two hands grabbed Arthur's collar and yanked the boy off his precarious perch. He landed on top of Sargon and both teens collapsed in a heap.

"You are mad as a top hat and in need of serious therapy." Sargon wrapped meaty arms round his quarry and held on. "This is a coward's way out."

"What are you talking about?" Arthur tried to wriggle free. "Get your hands off me!"

"You may think things are hopeless, but you have much to live for." Sargon tightened his grip. "Look at the wonders you will miss, such as hot dogs and Netflix. The tenth Avengers movie is coming out soon."

"Wait? What?" Arthur stopped struggling. "I'm not trying to *kill* myself."

"Of course not," Sargon replied sarcastically. "You are climbing onto this wall because you wish to do a Riverdance."

"I didn't come up here to commit suicide, you moron!" the boy snapped. "How desperate do you think I am?"

"On a scale of one to ten, I am presently putting you at eleven." Sargon squinted at his companion. "Why do you have a camera strapped onto your noggin?"

"That's why I wanted you to leave me on my own," Arthur spat. "I knew you wouldn't understand."

"You know nothing of the sort, for you have not even bothered to explain this insanity. You are agonising my leg but I am not letting go until you do."

"Stop moaning about your leg. I'd love to feel anything in mine. Even pain."

"Do not change the subject."

Arthur lapsed into a surly silence.

"Out with it," Sargon insisted. "We are not chummy enough for you to be sitting on my lap. If anyone comes up here, they will think we are cuddling and it will surely be bad for my reputation with the damsels."

"All right," Arthur said eventually. "I wanted to film myself hanging off a railing at the edge of the roof. Happy now?"

"Do not mistake my grimace for a cheesy grin. I am not understanding in the slightest."

"I'm trying to prove something, all right?"

"If you are trying to prove you can fly, I shall have to be educating you in the laws of physics."

Arthur gave an exasperated sigh.

"Have you ever heard of Parkour?" he asked.

"It is a type of floor." Sargon looked even more mystified. "What has that do with anything?"

"That's parquet. Parkour is also known as free running."

"Ah! This I have seen on YouTube, of which I am a big fan." Sargon snapped his fingers. "Those plucky fools are amazing. Jumping over things and leaping around and..."

"And hanging off buildings," Arthur finished. "I happen to be one of the best."

He sighed again and corrected himself.

"*Used* to be one of the best."

12

I have been asked to compile a short psychiatric evaluation on Arthur Lawson, a potential long-term patient at Collingwood Hospital.

Arthur's back was broken in a fall. Though the other injuries he sustained were fairly minor, his lower vertebra was sheared. The surgeons who operated on him say the damage to his spine is irreversible and he is now permanently confined to a wheelchair.

Arthur's history is not a happy one, I'm sorry to say. He idolised his parents who were sports enthusiasts and, sadly, died in a climbing accident several years ago. As a result, Arthur was brought up in Sunnyside State Home, just outside Edinburgh.

I contacted Sunnyside and had his case history transferred to me. It revealed a pattern of anti-social behaviour and risk taking. Unsurprisingly, Arthur developed a passion for extreme sports, especially those involving climbing. It is as if he wanted to emulate his dead parents, which is entirely understandable. Since he had no real outlet for this, he used the facility grounds as a homemade obstacle course and could often be found on the roof, after climbing out of the window and scaling the drainpipes. He also ran away several times, though he was always found and brought back.

Given his adventurous nature, Arthur took the news that he would never walk again particularly hard. Originally placed in New Collingwood Hospital, he was abrasive to the nurses, refused to eat for long periods of time and antagonised the patients. Visiting hours were particularly difficult, as Arthur had no other relatives and resented those who did. Eventually, he was moved to his own room on the 4th floor of Eden Heights.

It was at this point that I was brought in to assess his mental health and interviewed him on four separate occasions.

Though he seems lacking in empathy and rather manipulative, I found Arthur Lawson to be an exceptionally bright and imaginative boy. Perhaps too imaginative, for he seems to engage in confabulation. He contradicts the official report that he lacked the strength to hold on while attempting a dangerous stunt, insisting that the accident was caused by a faulty railing on the building he was climbing. He is also bitter *that the surgeons refused to carry out surgery which might have allowed him to walk again, an operation they considered too dangerous to perform.*

As he put it in one of our conversations.

"I'd have been willing to go ahead with it but was never asked. What right did they have to make that decision? Next time I break my back, I'm going private."

To me, this statement encapsulates Arthur Lawson. He is a daredevil who resents authority and covers up bitterness at the hand he has been dealt with sarcasm and black humour. But I suggest he be carefully monitored, for he is severely depressed, utterly bored and the accident has robbed him of all self-esteem.

My recommendation, in the short term, is that he be given a roommate. He needs someone his own age to talk to, for he is too smart and resentful to open up to a middle-aged therapist he knows is probing his psyche.

I would suggest another boy, one who has also had a difficult life and perhaps suffered trauma of another type. This may give Arthur a different perspective on his own situation.

To be honest, what he really needs is a friend.

13

"This is how you have such impressive arm muscles on your puny body." Sargon suddenly understood. "And how you hurt yourself too, I will wager."

"I sneaked onto the roof of the new hospital," Arthur conceded. "Was about to film myself doing a single handstand on the railings there. I don't remember what happened after that."

"I am not having to be a rock scientist to guess." Sargon pushed his companion off and struggled to his feet. "It is fortunate you were already at the hospital when you fell."

"Yeah. Lucky me."

"So what do you hope to demonstrate by dangling from a much higher building like a floppy monkey? That you can make the same mistake twice?"

"Everyone says I fell because I wasn't strong enough to perform the manoeuvre," Arthur replied vehemently. "That's bollocks, cause I practised for weeks. I say the railing gave way."

"And you are willing to risk your *life* showing they were in error."

"What's wrong with that?" Arthur stuck out his chin defiantly. "I'm not letting anyone get away with calling me a liar."

"And I am not letting you end up a bloody puddle on the ground." Sargon pointed the way they had come. "You are coming back with me right now, if I have to drag you by the ears."

"All right, already!" Arthur held up his hands in surrender. "That's not the only reason I have for being up here."

"Is this excuse equally dim?"

"There's an online Parkour competition and it ends in a few days." The teen thumped his useless legs. "If I can film myself hanging off a twenty storey building in a lightning storm with pins that don't work, then haul myself back again, I'll win for sure."

"Ah. So it is even *more* stupid."

"The prize is £50,000."

Sargon's eyebrows shot up.

"Suddenly I am thinking you are making plenty of sense."

"You know it," Arthur said bitterly. "Without that money, what will happen to me? I'll be stuck in hospital forever or left rotting in some home with no family and friends."

"*I* am willing to be your friend," Sargon said awkwardly. "And would have been sooner if you had told me the truth in the first place."

"The truth is that people believe I'm a useless lump of flesh." Arthur shook his head miserably. "They look right through the person and see an object instead."

"This is easily done," Sargon agreed. "I have witnessed it with my own eyes."

"Then help me prove them wrong," Arthur pleaded. "Lower me so I can drop onto that parapet. I'll crawl to the damned edge if I have to."

Sargon leaned over the wall, mentally measuring the distance.

"I am doubting a person with good legs would land properly," he argued. "Yours will surely crumple like pieces of paper. You will then put out your arms to break the fall and they will shatter too. I doubt you can hang from the railing by your teeth."

Arthur seemed like he might object. Only he knew in his heart that Sargon was right.

"But ponder on this." The teen tapped his lip. "You say there are still a few days before your contest to find the world's biggest idiot finishes?"

"Not making me feel better."

"Then perhaps we can find a new way to win, for I am a tremendously inventive individual." He gave a wolfish grin. "And, of course, you would then be giving me half the prize money."

"Is that why we're mates all of a sudden?"

"Do not be silly." Sargon looked offended. "If we were not buddies, I would be asking for 70%."

"Short of building a catapult and firing me into Edinburgh," Arthur snorted. "I don't see how I've got much of a chance now."

"I have already considered this," Sargon replied solemnly. "But the elastic in my underwear is old and worn."

"You won't make me laugh, so stop trying."

"The age of my undies is no matter for giggling. I long for a sexy pair of Calvin Klein's like I have seen in their creepy black and white adverts."

"Well, I'm not lending you mine. It takes forever for me to get them off."

"Then, right now, I am thinking we should get out of here before we are found out. Back in our whiffy room, we can do some barn storming."

He picked up the vase and plonked it on Arthur's knee.

"Be careful with that," the boy warned. "The lid has come loose."

A huge burst of wind billowed across the roof. The top of the urn tumbled off and a swirling cloud of ash enveloped Sargon.

"I am covered in dead person!" The boy staggered backwards, swiping at his face. "I may have bits of bum in my mouth!"

He lost his balance and landed flat on his back. Arthur gave a loud guffaw.

"I thought you were never intending to laugh again?" Sargon grumped, picking grit from his teeth.

"So did I. But no matter how often you fall over, it never gets old."

The laugh drifted into a stifled sob.

"I'm well aware I'll never walk another step, Sargon. I just wanted to feel a bit like my old self. Understand?"

"I did not know your old self." Sargon sat up. "But the person you are now is not such a bad sort, I suppose."

"All right. Let's go back." Arthur gave a loud sniff and wiped his eyes. "You kept your end of the bargain, so fair's fair. I'll ask to be moved and you can have my room, even if it's only for a week."

"I must be honest too," Sargon said guiltily. "I had intended to flee the hospital tonight while you were up here. I am expecting visitors I most certainly do not wish to receive."

"What kind of visitors?"

"From the immigration authorities," the boy said morosely. "I am illegally in this country, you see."

"Ah." Arthur caught on immediately. "*That's* why you wanted your own room in the Eyesore."

"Indeed. The staff have been ordered not to let me leave and it is hard to sneak away from a ward full of people, with a full complement of nurses watching. Or a room with a nosey neighbour."

"But if I were on the roof…"

"It would make things easier, yes."

"Sneaky," Arthur said. "But you looked out for me so it's only right I do the same. When we get back, take off and I'll cover for you as long as I can."

He reached out his hand.

"You'll be long gone before anyone realises. I'm an excellent liar."

"For what it is worth, I might have enjoyed sharing a room with you." This time, Sargon accepted the boy's help. "With negative TV, I would sorely be needing someone to annoy for entertainment."

Once upright, he took hold of the wheelchair handles and began to push Arthur towards the exit.

"While we're being honest," Arthur said. "Your funny accent and misuse of words is fake, isn't it? Why are you...?"

Sargon suddenly stopped.

"Ehm... There may be a spanner in our works." He nodded towards the concrete structure they had emerged from.

A gust of wind had blown the door shut. The brick lay a few feet away.

"This is v. unfortunate." Sargon reached the door and leaned against it to rest his leg. "If we are stuck up here all night, with a storm rapidly approaching, we shall be icy pops by morning."

There was a dull whump from somewhere below them, like a giant fist hitting a punching bag. A startled gull took off from its perch on the scaffolding, screeching in protest before fading to a tiny speck. The glow emanating from each skylight flickered and dimmed before returning to normal.

"What the hell was that?" Arthur asked. "Is there someone on the top floor?"

"Arthur," Sargon whispered. "We have to get off this roof."

"I know that. It's going to get a lot colder as night falls."

"I mean, we must do it without the slightest delay."

"Why? What's going on, buddy?"

"I recognise that terrible sound," Sargon said grimly. "For I have heard it many times before."

"It was just a bang," Arthur replied uncertainly. "So what?"

"No." There was no trace of doubt in his companion's voice.

"What we heard was most definitely an explosion."

14

"Aw, don't be dumb." Arthur patted his friend's arm. "It was probably a car engine backfiring somewhere."

"Please be quiet." Sargon held up a hand. "And put a prick up your ears."

"We'll have to work on your vocabulary later," Arthur giggled. "Right now, I don't hear anything but the approaching storm."

"There is a different storm coming, I am thinking. Listen with more carefulness."

The boys waited until the gale abated for a few seconds. Now they could detect a faint ringing.

"That is a fire alarm. I fear something has gone terribly wrong downstairs."

"Let's not hang around then." Arthur leaned forwards and tugged on the handle. "It's locked, right enough. We'll have to break it open."

"I am hoping this may do the trick." Sargon bent carefully and picked up the brick. "Stand back. Or... sit back, I mean."

He began to hammer at the lock.

"It is not in the mood for budging." He continued to pound, holding the wall to keep from toppling over again. "Why is the lock so strong? This is a hospital roof, not Guantanamo Bay."

"It's always been a prison to me," Arthur grunted. "Wouldn't really care if it went up in smoke - just not when I'm on the bloody top."

"I could film that on your camera." Sargon gave a wry grin. "You whizzing around while burning like a Roman Catholic candle would surely win first prize in our competition."

"Oh, it's *our* competition now?"

"Perhaps you should be writing out your will, just in case." Sargon tapped the notebook in his pocket. "You may leave everything you possess to me. I do not want the urn."

"Glad to see you're getting your sense of humour back."

"I am likely to poo myself from terror but you have had enough bad luck and I wish to keep your pecker up."

"Not quite the correct phrase as usual, but I appreciate the sentiment. What are you going to leave *me*?"

"Unless you desire a lifetime of bad memories," Sargon said cryptically, "I have nothing to offer."

"Let me see if I can find something to help." Arthur wheeled away. "With all this demolition work going on, there must be tools lying around."

"Do that. I shall continue with my sorry efforts."

Sargon went back to beating on the lock. After five minutes, he gave up. The door was made of steel and the lock was just as tough. The boy's leg was throbbing, even though he had made no headway.

Arthur suddenly appeared, holding a crowbar.

"Always wanted to do this," he said. "Never thought I'd get the chance."

He wedged the bar into the crack between door and wall and pulled. It didn't budge.

"You did not happen to find dynamite on your travels?" Sargon mopped his brow. "Because nothing else will open this, I am thinking."

"Looks like we're stuck then." Arthur looked uncertain, "If there really is a fire, though, someone will come to get us. Won't they?"

"I left a note saying we were going to the hospital grounds, remember?" Sargon corrected. "The building will surely be evacuated, toot sweet, and everyone will be thinking we are already outside." He slapped his forehead. "I have been too clever for my own clogs."

"What if we threw a hammer or something off the side? That would get everyone's attention."

"Especially if it landed on a nurse's head. This we cannot risk, even if it is only massive Doreen."

"Will you *stop* fat shaming Doreen?"

"I thought I was merely describing her."

"I'll find some way to signal we're up here." Arthur wasn't the type to accept defeat. "Make a kind of flag, perhaps. Or even…"

"It may not matter that we are detected," Sargon interrupted. "If the situation is bad, the fire brigade will concentrate all their efforts on putting it out rather than risking men and resources trying to reach the roof."

"What? You're an expert on emergency procedures all of a sudden?"

"As a matter of fact, I have an exceptionally fine grasp in that area," the teen replied tersely. "And I have seen a whole town burn around me."

"They can send a helicopter. Lift us off."

"Where would it land?" Sargon swept his hand in an arc. "The entire roof is covered in plastic and steel nastiness."

"Couldn't they let down some kind of harness?" Confidence was draining from Arthur's voice.

"It is blowing like a tuba from all directions and this storm will only grow in magnitude. Soon they will have trouble just staying in the air."

"Anyone ever mention what a party pooper you are?"

"I am a practical fellow," Sargon repeated. "I have said so many times."

"What do you suggest then?" Arthur asked. "Sit here and hope someone can put out the fire?"

"In my country, people usually die while waiting to be rescued." The boy handed Arthur his crowbar and stumped off. "It will most certainly not happen to me. We must seize our bollocks by their horns."

A minute later, he was staggering back, pulling a workman's ladder.

"Hey!" Arthur complained. "I could have used that to get down onto the parapet."

"This is why I did not tell you I had found it," Sargon replied shrewdly. "You and I can have a tiff later if we have not shuffled off our mortal coil."

"That's never going to reach the ground," Arthur tutted. "It's about 150 feet too short."

"I am glad you have also held onto your funny bone. But it will reach what I want it to."

A few yards away was the plastic cover of a skylight. Sargon picked up the crowbar, inserted it under the edge and yanked. The shell lifted with a creak and he pulled it loose, throwing the covering aside.

An acrid smell wafted up, before being whipped away by the wind. Now they could hear the alarm properly.

"I'd say we were officially screwed, buddy." Arthur tapped the camera on his head. "I'm still recording if you have any last words."

"Any last words I have will be said to my foxy nurse when I am ninety years old." Sargon slid the ladder through the gap until it reached the floor of the offices below. "Those I will most certainly not be wanting captured on film."

He manoeuvred himself carefully onto the top rung and slowly descended, trying to keep weight off his injured foot.

"I shall go to a window and shout for assistance."

"They don't open and you can't break the glass, re-member? It's reinforced with wire and the panes are filthy. Nobody will see or hear you twenty floors up."

"That is exceedingly poor planning and I shall be writing to the management." Sargon finally reached the ground. "Let me try anyway."

Arthur listened to his companion moving around. There were several loud thumps and a lot of cursing.

"You are right." The teen's voice drifted up. "I can-not even dent it."

"Office phones?"

"They must have been removed to the new build-ing." Sargon appeared below, looking apprehensive. "And old elevators are too dangerous to use during a fire, so I have no choice but to attempt the stairs."

"Even if they're passable, you'd have to limp down twenty flights to get help." Arthur curled his lip. "If I don't burn, I'll starve to bloody death before you can send a rescue party."

"I know it will not be eating a piece of cake," Sar-gon retorted angrily. "Do you have a better idea?"

"I sure as hell do. I'm coming with you."

"That is foolish talk. How will you manage to get down this ladder for starters?"

"Using my arms. I told you they were strong."

"And then I carry you the rest of the way? With my leg in a cast?"

"We're in a hospital. There's a wheelchair on every floor."

"You cannot be taking a wheelchair down the stairs."

"I'll find a way, don't you worry." The boy began to inch out of his chair and onto the gravel surface of the roof. "Leave me behind if you want. I'll follow along at my own pace."

Sargon dug fingers into his palms.

"I am a sensible chap, as we both know," he said. "You must stay up there so the firemen will know exactly where you are."

"I don't see how you can stop me." Arthur reached for the ladder.

Sargon pushed it over and it landed with a crash, sending up a cloud of dust.

"Sargon!" Arthur cried. "What are you doing?"

"You have my word that I shall fetch assistance. I will not let another boy die."

"What do you mean *another* boy?"

"I will explain when we are saved. You do not have to be afraid."

"I'm not afraid! I was trying to hang off the edge of the damned building a few minutes ago."

"I am truly sorry." Sargon turned away. "But it is for your own good and I am not having time to argue."

"You complete dick! This is how everyone treats me!"

Arthur lay on the roof shouting into the hole.

"I thought we were *friends*."

But Sargon was gone.

-Part 2-

Some women fear the fire. Some women simply become it...

R. H. Sin

Part 2

15

Statement by Doreen Jones, nurse at
Old Collingwood Hospital

I was about to do my late rounds when there was a loud boom and the fire alarm went off. In the event of an emergency, our first priority is to evacuate the building. There weren't many staff on that night but nor were there a lot of patients left in Old Collingwood. None were in critical condition, so it was fairly easy to get everyone out.

Even so, I went around the occupied wards to make sure we hadn't missed any patients. When I got to Arthur Lawson's room, it was empty, which I thought was unusual, as he doesn't ever leave. Then I found a note from his new roommate, Sargon Danaan. It said he and Arthur had gone outside and would be back later.

I had no idea it was a lie.

Not long after we emptied the building, fire engines arrived and there was a lot of confusion. I couldn't see the boys but after reading their note I wasn't worried. After all, Arthur was in a wheelchair and Sargon had a cast. It never occurred to me that they might still be inside, never mind on the roof.

I am so sorry. I should have kept searching until I found them.

If I had, Sargon might still be alive.

16

Sargon hobbled out of the office and along the passageway towards the stairs, leaning on the wall to propel himself. The smell of smoke was stronger now, convincing him he had made the right decision. The most realistic course of action was to proceed alone. If he waited for his companion, it would take forever for them to descend.

He could have left Arthur to make his own way down, but there was no telling how far the determined boy would get - and that would complicate matters further. There were stairs at either end of the Eyesore. If Sargon found firemen and they *were* able to make it to the top, they might take a different route from Arthur and go right past him.

Yet he still felt deeply ashamed.

He reached the elevator and licked his lips. It would be so easy to take that to the ground but there was no way to tell exactly where the fire was located.

But there was one thing he *was* sure of. The Eyesore was old and the lift probably dated back to before modern safety features were invented. Which meant it would short circuit if encountering intense heat and stop on the affected floor. The doors would open onto the conflagration, incinerating anyone inside before they closed again.

Sargon shuddered at the thought.

He heard the faint wail of sirens outside, which meant the fire brigade had arrived. As soon as they entered the building, the firemen would shut off the elevators completely - to stop anyone making that very mistake.

This was his last chance. Perhaps he could risk taking the lift down five or six floors. Every second counted, after all. Yet the haze indicated a fire was close.

His finger hovered near the button.

"No," he muttered. "You have not lived this long by being slap-happy and haberdash."

He passed the lift, carried on to the stairwell and pushed open the fire door.

A cloud of pungent smoke billowed up, making his eyes water. Covering his mouth with one hand, he began to descend, holding onto the handrail. An orange glow emanated from below and he could hear a sound like a thousand sheets of paper crumpling.

Sargon leaned over the railing and gasped in horror.

The landing beneath him was engulfed. Paint was peeling from the walls and floating upwards like tiny glow worms. The intense heat instantly scorched his face.

The boy jerked his head back.

"I fear my eyebrows are gone," he muttered, trying to stay calm. "Now I shall have to turn off the camera when Skyping foxy ladies."

He turned and hurried back towards the opposite stairwell, hoping it was still clear. The boy moved along the passage as fast as he could manage, half running, half skipping.

Turning a corner, he stopped, not sure if he could believe his eyes.

At the far end of the corridor stood a nurse. She was bent over, both hands clasping her knees, gasping for breath. After a few seconds, she straightened up and strode towards him.

As she grew closer, Sargon's brow furrowed.

The nurse didn't appear to be any older than him. A grubby hat with a scarlet cross sat at a precarious angle on her tangle of thick red hair and she was bathed in perspiration.

"You appear to be somewhat flustered." Sargon decided questions about her age could wait. "Did you ascend the far stairs by any chance?"

"Just ran up fifteen flights," she panted. "Give me a minute."

Sargon studied her. The girl was tall and slender, with wide green eyes and a rash of freckles. She smelled strongly of smoke and the edges of her outfit were singed. She coughed loudly and wiped her mouth with a trembling hand.

"Your sooty appearance is causing me grave concern." Sargon tried not to sound as alarmed as he felt. "Please inform me of the situation below immediately."

"Bad fire in two places," the girl said. "Fifth and sixth floors and a couple of levels down too. I barely made it past."

"Can we be getting back down that way?"

"Doubt it. Where's your friend?"

"Arthur is still on the roof," Sargon said. "But he is in a wheelchair."

"I'll get him." The girl waved him away. "Take the stairs at the other end. We'll catch up."

"This I have already attempted, to no avail." Sargon glanced over his shoulder where dirty grey tendrils were snaking along the roof. "It is a flaming mess in the most literal sense."

The teen bit his lip.

"I am hoping you have at least alerted the authorities as to our dire predicament."

"Didn't see anyone," the girl wheezed. "Hardly any staff on this time of night."

"Then dial 999 on your mobile, idiotic female!"

"Don't have one."

"You do not have one?" The boy stared at her in disbelief. "There are nomads in the desert who have smartphones."

"I don't."

"Where exactly did you run here from? The 19th century?"

"Don't harp on." The stranger doubled over again, racked by another bout of coughing. "Won't change anything."

"And you will not be missed in the evacuation, will you?" Sargon pressed. "For you are not a real nurse, I will wager. Not unless you passed your exams when you were twelve."

"I sneak into the building at night," The girl replied defiantly. "Help myself to food and get warm. If I pass anyone, I keep my head down and they only see the uniform."

"Ah. I also know what it is like to be homeless," Sargon replied sympathetically. "You do what you must to get by."

He gave a sardonic grin.

"I presume you are toasty enough now."

"Less chat." The girl finally regained her breath. "Let's fetch your pal."

"Come on then, utterly useless saviour." Sargon clumped off. "Though I am not looking forward to telling Arthur that we are likely to be roasted like Thanksgiving turkeys."

"You always this ungrateful?" The girl followed, glowering at him. "Fifteen damned flights I came up."

"Forgive me." Sargon was suddenly abashed. "Terror has put feet in my mouth. At least you are trying to rescue us."

"Yeah. I was a fool."

The boy wasn't sure if she was talking about coming to their aid alone or coming to their aid at all. He decided to be more diplomatic.

"I am called Sargon Danaan," he said. "Do I address you as sister or matron?"

"Courage." She took his arm and marched him along the passage. "Courage Louviere."

"That is indeed an... unusual name. What were your parents thinking?"

"I'm not much of a talker, Sargon."

"Fair enough."

They reached the roof stairs and Courage helped the boy to the top.

"Arthur may be in a rather bad mood and I fear our news will not improve his temperament." Sargon pushed the bar on the emergency door and hobbled out onto the roof.

"Arthur!" he shouted. "I am back and have brought a friend called Courage. She is the strong silent type."

"About bloody time." Arthur wheeled around the concrete block. "Not that I needed you. I found these and was just about to make short work of the door."

A jackhammer and axe were balanced on his lap

"This is your mate?" Courage asked. "I like him,"

"So, what happened?" Arthur said grumpily. "I thought you'd be half way down the building by now and fetching the cavalry."

"Nobody is coming." Courage looked around. "Floors five, six and eighteen are on fire."

"Our new comrade does not mince up words," Sargon said. "This is probably for the best, as she would also be telling you nobody knows we are here."

"Won't *you* be missed, though?" Arthur looked at her carefully. "Wait a minute. You're pretty young to be a nurse."

"Courage is currently between addresses, so her wardrobe is limited," Sargon said. "But she has two legs that work, so do not be looking a gift horse in the dentures."

"Sorry," Arthur apologised. "And thank you for…"

"Where's my urn?" The girl interrupted.

"*Your* urn?" Sargon blanched. "Did we steal a dead relation?"

"I doubt it," Arthur said resentfully. "She probably wants the big wad of money I found hidden under the ash."

"That's right."

"Why was it in *there*?" Sargon looked confused.

"My hedge fund manager has the day off."

"You need a home to open a bank account," Arthur pointed out. "If you don't have one, a funeral urn in a disused cupboard is as good a place as any to hide valuables. After all, who would nick that?"

"That's what I thought." Courage replied resentfully.

"So you did not come up here to save us?" Sargon's face fell. "You were simply intent on retrieving your ashy cash?"

"It's my life savings." The girl held out her hand.

"Then you may have it… if you help in getting us to safety." Sargon looked to Arthur for support. "I saw fire extinguishers on the wall that we can use to get past the fire."

"I already blackmailed *you* into helping me, Sargon." Arthur dug a hand in his pocket. "I won't make the same mistake twice."

"I am certainly not so finicky. Once our fake rescuer has the dosh, I wager we will not see her shapely backside for dust."

"Here." Arthur pulled out a pile of bills in a plastic bag and handed it to Courage. "It's all there."

"Thanks." The girl took the money and stuffed it in her pocket. "Let's go. The aggravating guy is right. Extinguishers are our best bet."

"Ah. You are not going to take off and leave us, after all." Sargon blushed. "I am suddenly wishing a hole would open in the ground and swallow me up."

"We don't get moving?" Courage retorted. "That might actually happen."

17

Brandon Gollege stuck his head out the window of the fire truck and let the wind rush through his shock of blonde hair. At nineteen, he was the youngest member of Lothian and Borders Fire and Rescue service and this was his first emergency.

He didn't want the others to know it, but he was drying perspiration from his face. He was excited but also afraid. Scared of screwing up on his first mission. Scared of not measuring up to expectations.

And, yes, afraid of getting killed.

But he couldn't let the others see that. To them, he was 'Puppy'. Eager, earnest and ready for action.

"Wind your neck in and stick a helmet on." Bailly Cousins pulled him back onto the seat and shut the window. "It's bloody freezing."

Cousins was a station officer with a black band on his white helmet denoting the rank.

"Could be a big one, though, eh? It's in Eden Heights, the old part of Collingwood Hospital. The building they call the Eyesore." Nerves made Brandon even more chatty than normal. "That's, like, twenty stories high, isn't it?"

"A fire alarm went off, is all. Don't get your knickers in a twist."

"We'll probably be back at the station in half an hour," the driver of the vehicle spun the steering wheel and rocketed round a corner. Sally 'Tyres' Hampton was one of the few women on the force and, despite only being in her twenties, was already a veteran of seven emergencies.

"Especially at the speed you drive." Bailly slammed a yellow hard hat on Brandon's head. "We're more likely to die in a head-on collision than any blaze."

Tyres grinned and pressed harder on the accelerator.

The radio crackled to life and a soft Caledonian voice filled the cab.

This is Deputy Chief Markham Silver. Are you there, Officer Cousins? Over.

Bailly and Tyres glanced at each other. Markham was a high-ranking officer. There was no way he would be involved in a routine call-out.

Their suspicions were quickly confirmed.

We're getting reports of an explosion at Eden Heights. Floors five and six are on fire, last I heard. What's your position and ETA?

Bailly grabbed the mike.

"We're on the A8 about five minutes away. Benson is off sick, so there's only three of us in the truck. But the second response vehicle is right behind us."

I've put out an alert to other stations in Edinburgh and requested additional support, but you're the closest unit.

Brandon felt the hairs on the back of his neck rise. This was it. He was in the thick of things. He still wasn't sure how he felt about that.

"What are your orders, Sir?" Bailly asked.

Fortunately, the situation isn't nearly as bad as it might be. None of the floors above four are occupied and, according to the staff, all patients have been evacuated and accounted for. Nobody is in danger, so there's no need for heroics.

The occupants of the cab were delighted by this bit of news. Saving human lives was their priority and rescuing survivors was the action that put fire-fighters at most risk. They would try to save the building of course, but it was only bricks and mortar.

"I'll set up a perimeter and make sure all civilians are at a safe distance," Bailly said. "Get any police officers there to enforce it."

Do that. Other engines will be arriving soon and I'll be there in twenty minutes. Until then, you take the lead. Over.

"We'll check the basement first, then set up an anchor point. Over and out."

He turned to Brandon and winked.

"It's your lucky day, Puppy. A real honest-to-goodness situation."

Brandon mentally went over his training. The worst thing that could happen to a fireman was to be trapped above a blaze. So first port of call was checking the basement for flammable material and clearing it away.

Next came the anchor point. Men would ascend the stairs with their hoses, breaking the window panes to ventilate the area and clear away smoke. On reaching the blaze, they would hold firm, pouring water on the flames. Once they had the upper hand, they could slowly proceed, dousing the flames until the fire was out. It was a tried and tested method.

They crested the rise of the hill and Tyres drew a sharp breath.

"Crap. There's more than one fire."

The outline of Eden Heights was plainly visible in the fading light, two of the lower floors glowing, licks of orange pulsing behind the windows. And the same horrible lambency was emanating near the top.

"Put a spurt on Tyres." Bally's face was grim. "It's worse than we thought."

The truck careened into the open square in front of the Eyesore, bumping onto a grass verge. The trio leapt out as a second, larger engine drew up behind. A crowd of hospital staff and patients were gathered twenty yards away, some wrapped in blankets. Tongues of flame were now leaping from the fifth floor windows, illuminating the scene with a ghastly orange tint.

Three police cars were already on the scene, lights flashing. Bailly beckoned to an officer.

"Move those vehicles and send all evacuees to the main hospital. Make sure everyone stays indoors."

"Shouldn't we get everyone out of there too?" The man looked doubtful. "What if the fire spreads?"

"No. It's a safe distance," the Station Officer explained. "What we don't need is several thousand more people milling around, freezing their arses off and adding to this confusion."

"Will do." The policeman took off.

Bailly approached his fire-fighters unreeling hoses from the second cab.

"Noakes? Extend the ladders on your engine as far as they'll go. Target the windows you can reach. Nothing we can do about the fire up top for now."

"I'm on it."

"Tyres. Into the basement. Radio on. You know what to look for. Take Puppy with you."

As they turned to go, Bailly grabbed Brandon's arm.

"Stay calm and remember what you've been taught." He gave a reassuring squeeze.

"You'll be fine."

Brandon and Tyres jogged through the deserted entrance hall and down the stairs. Four ambulances slumbered in the underground parking bay. Tyres switched on her walkie-talkie.

"Bailly. Find some paramedics and have them drive the emergency vehicles out of the basement."

Brandon understood immediately. It was likely the ambulances were topped up after each journey, which meant they had full tanks of petrol. If they were to catch fire, each vehicle would be turned into a miniature bomb.

Fortunately, there were only three or four cars, since it was outside visiting hours and most of the staff had gone home. Those would have to stay. Apart from that, there was nothing too dangerous in the concrete bay. Tyres gave a satisfied nod.

"Next floor." She trotted down another flight of stairs, Brandon close behind.

This was the sub-basement and it was a different matter entirely. The roof was low and the corridors led off to rooms and alcoves of various sizes, each a potential hazard. Brandon and Tyres began opening them, taking a silent inventory. Oil drums for the heating system. Containers of cleaning fluid. Shelves full of paper towels and toilet rolls. Every kind of hospital supply imaginable. In one of the larger rooms, they found giant garbage bins overflowing with cardboard and rags, stinking to high heaven. Too much to clear out without an army of helpers. If the fire ever got down here, it would quickly turn into an inferno.

"There's one ray of light." Brandon nudged Tyres and pointed. Lined up outside the door of a service elevator, like robotic toy soldiers, were a dozen fire extinguishers, ready to be relocated.

"Spares, I suppose," the woman acknowledged. "Be a lot more use if they were on the bloody wards."

They had reached the end of the last corridor and were facing three final doors. Brandon tried the first but it was locked. The second was a large storeroom full of medical supplies.

Tyres went through the third door and cursed loudly.

This was the boiler room. All three furnaces were turned to maximum and the temperature was so high it caused the air to shimmer. She moved quickly from one to the other, shutting them down, watching as the pressure gauges dropped from red to zero.

Brandon rounded the back of one huge copper cylinder and frowned.

"You better come see, Sally."

The wall was lined with banks of blackened fuse boxes. Tyres cursed loudly and pulled out her radio.

"You there, Bailly? Over."

Always. What's the story?

"No immediate danger, thank God. But the lower basement is a tinderbox. More worryingly, the fuse boxes are ruined but the backup generator hasn't kicked in."

Can you turn it on from down there?

"You're missing the point. Everything is still working."

Explain.

"If the main fuse box is in this state, it must have been overloaded. Which means it should have blown and cut the power." Tyres prided herself on a knowledge of electrical systems, a definite advantage in her line of work. "I'll bet the normal fuse wire has been replaced by something too thick to be effective."

There was a pause at the other end.

Which can't be good news.

"That's an understatement. Any bit of badly insulated wiring in this building may have been melted by the surge. I imagine that's what started the blaze near the top."

So, there could be a number of small electrical fires smouldering throughout the structure? Is that what you're saying?

"That's what I'm saying, Bailly. This place is a sodding death trap."

18

"I'll bump you down to the floor below," Courage told Arthur. "Then you'll have to wait."

"We will try to put out the burning stairwell," Sargon added. "And come back for you once it is done."

"Ditch the tools." Courage took hold of the wheelchair handles. "This thing looks difficult enough to manage."

"Just slow down a minute," Arthur said. "If the fire is that bad, we need to consider our options."

"It's not a discussion," Courage reached for the jackhammer and tried to yank it away from the boy. "Let go."

"*Think* you two." Arthur held on to the tool. "You might put out the fire in the stairwell but where was it coming from in the first place?"

"The whole corridor is burning, that's where," Courage scowled. "Idiot workmen removed the fire doors to get equipment in, I suppose. Saw it as I went past."

"So…. even if you put out the stairwell, it'll probably catch light again by the time you come back up to help me."

"This is indeed true," Sargon said glumly. "We are in a cloud without a silver lining and no mistaking."

"You need to leave me behind." Arthur finally allowed Courage to take the jackhammer. "I'll stick it out here until you send help. Again."

Sargon swallowed hard. There was a time when he would have taken off without a second thought. But he was not that person any more.

"Sargon Danaan does not leave a friend behind." He squeezed Arthur's shoulder. "Please come up with a better plan."

"All right." Arthur scanned the rooftop. "When I did Parkour, I never tried any kind of stunt without knowing the terrain inside out."

"You did Parkour?" Courage whistled. "That's cool."

"And you've been prowling around this hospital without getting caught for who knows how long." Arthur turned to her. "You must know the layout pretty well."

"I do."

"The top floors have management offices. But what else is up here? Especially on the burning floor."

"Surgeon's consulting rooms. Thousands of patient records. Kitchen and restaurant for management and senior doctors, with a ton of food supplies and drums of cooking oil. All ready to be moved to the new hospital. Storage fridges and cupboards."

She paused.

"I glanced down the corridor and saw the doors to all the rooms were closed, but it won't take long for the flames to get through them."

"Apparently, you're an expert on fires." Arthur thumped Sargon. "What's the worst-case scenario, given what you've heard?"

"Once the blaze reaches the patient records rooms, those files will go up like… eh… paper." Sargon ticked his fingers. "The fireball will burst through to the offices and kitchen and make the containers explode. These will cause an inferno which will quickly engulf the top floor and then the roof."

He winced.

"The burning cooking oil will also flow down the stairs, igniting everything in its path. Either way, we are up a creek without paddling."

"Sorry I asked," Arthur gulped.

"Unless…" Sargon thought hard. "We put out the existing fire in one swoop."

"With hand held extinguishers?" Courage raised an eyebrow. "Not possible."

"What about that?" Sargon pointed to the wooden tower at the edge of the roof. "Is it not a water receptacle of some sort?"

"It'll be empty," Arthur said regretfully. "Most likely a throwback from when the Eyesore was built, for supplying water to the upper floors. But everything must be piped up from the basement these days."

"No," Courage corrected. "It's still used to fill the swimming pool on the level below."

"Management has a swimming pool?" Arthur shook his head. "Are you *kidding* me?"

"Got a gym too."

"Do not flap your gums further about this," Sargon warned the girl. "Or Arthur's head is likely to take off into space with indignation."

"Not today." The boy studied the tank. "This is something we could use to our advantage."

"There's a valve on the bottom," Courage pointed. "But the water will come out too slowly to be any use."

"Perhaps we can get round that." The boy smiled slyly. "Though it will be risky."

"Aha! Arthur is doing his thinky thing," Sargon grinned. "And he is a very resourceful sort."

"Plus I've had plenty of time to scope out the roof," Arthur said. "Y'know. After you abandoned me."

"Shall I offer up my kisser for you to punch or will a swift kick in the nethers do?" Sargon stuck out his bottom. "Then we can agree that this is water under our troubled bridge and get back to staying alive."

"Aw, get your ass out of my face." The boy slapped Sargon's rump. "Do you trust me or not?"

"Trusting you got me here." Sargon straightened up. "Surely I must have faith you will get me back."

Arthur winked at the girl.

"Courage? What are your thoughts?"

"Too deep for you to understand."

"Oooh!" Sargon blew on his fingers. "You are already scorched, Arthur, and we have not even started our journey."

"We need to start working together as a team, Courage. Play to our strengths."

"Didn't say no, did I?"

"You're the only one who's properly mobile." Arthur waved her away. "Go search the pool area and gymnasium. I need goggles and anything else floaty. Inflatable armbands would be best. And helmets. Elbow pads. Any protective equipment a sportsman might use."

"Will do."

"Open the doors to the offices too."

"All right."

"And take the jackhammer. It's gas powered, so it works without a compressor."

"Ok."

"You really don't talk much, do you?"

"Nope."

"Sargon? You go with her. Courage will hand over the jackhammer when you get there."

"You *do* have a plan," the boy beamed. "What will I be doing with that fine implement?"

"Start punching holes in the floor, through to the fire below."

"And it is a terrible plan." The boy threw up his hands. "What is your part in all this while I am being sizzled like an unwilling hog?"

"I'm the guy telling you what to do. Nice to be management for a change."

"It is a shoe that certainly fits," Sargon shot back. "You have been my boss for five seconds and already power has gone to your head. You are setting me up to be crispy fries."

"Three or four holes, right in the middle," Arthur insisted. "Then get back here."

"You are enjoying this entirely too much, my friend."

"You know it." The boy's grin widened. "I never get to do anything exciting."

"C'mon then." Courage beckoned to Sargon. "And quit whining."

"No wonder the NHS is going down the tubes." Sargon took the axe from Arthur to use as a crutch. "You are having an appalling bedside manner."

"Oh, I'm sorry." Courage put on a look of fake concern. "How did you hurt your leg, Mr Danaan?"

"I was skiing in the Alps and collided with a farmer."

"Don't care. Let's go."

"Wonderful. I am trusting my continued existence to an uncaring supervisor and Hitler in a skirt."

He shambled after the girl and they vanished down the stairs.

19

On the nineteenth floor, the haze was noticeably thicker. Courage pulled a pair of surgical masks from her pocket and thrust one into Sargon's hand.

"Put it on," she said. "Might help,"

"As will this." Sargon took the mask and handed her the axe. "Break the windows as you go searching."

"They're wire latticed," she reminded him. "You can't smash them."

"Making small holes will be better than nothing. The cold air outside will suck out the smoke. It is called venting."

"All right." Courage ran off. Soon he could hear the sound of panes cracking.

"I am betting you are enjoying that," he murmured. "You seem like an exceedingly angry young woman."

Sargon switched on the jackhammer and began to drill. The vibrations sent a wave of pain through his leg and his teeth chattered uncontrollably. Then the tiles cracked and gave way. Within seconds, he was through.

A scarlet flush emanated from the hole.

"I was not expecting to see hell until I died." He moved on a few feet and began again. "Though that is

likely to occur much sooner than I would have pre-
ferred."

He was on the fourth puncture when Courage came
back, carrying a sports bag filled with equipment.

"Every part of me is tender from exertion." Sargon
switched off the jackhammer. "I shall be hoping for a
soothing massage when we reach safety."

"I'm not a real nurse, remember?"

"And I am not a real construction worker." Sargon
wiped his brow. "My arms are dropping off like flies
and I am getting very hot and bothered."

Vortexes of fire were beginning to creep over the
rim of the holes he had made, vainly seeking purchase
on the tiled floor.

"That's enough." Courage took his arm. "Let's go."

When they reached the roof, the girl emptied her
bag at Arthur's feet.

"Put everything on," he said. "Quick as you can."

They did so, then stood back and looked at each
other. Each wore knee and elbow pads, jock straps,
cricket helmets, swimming goggles and inflatable armbands.

"We are resembling the world's most ludicrous superheroes," Sargon struck a heroic pose. "I shall be
calling myself Captain Hopeless."

"That name's gonna stick, you know," Arthur sniggered.

"Wish I *had* a mobile," Courage said. "Wouldn't mind a selfie of this."

The boys stared at her.

"What? I can't make a joke too?"

"If imminent death brings out your fun side, who are we to complain?" Arthur pointed to the water tank. "That's what will save us."

"I do not want to be popping your enthusiastic bubbles," Sargon objected. "But Courage has already stated that the valve will let out water too slowly."

"I figured." Arthur wheeled across to a mound covered in plastic sheeting. "So we're going to pull it over."

He tugged away the sheet, revealing a crane like structure with a winch attached.

"Know what this is?"

"It's a davit," Courage said. "A mobile crane. The workmen must have bolted it to the roof for moving scaffolding around."

"Thank God the place is getting dismantled." Arthur nodded at a ladder attached to the side of the water tank. "Courage? Climb up there and attach the hook to the top. I've unwound the cable and it looks like it's just long enough to reach."

"Nice one." The girl took one end and headed for the ladder.

"Prise off the rest of the skylights, Sargon," Arthur added. "We've got to have as much water flowing to the floors below as possible. It'll drop through the holes you made onto the fire and go down the stairwells too."

"There must be twenty thousand gallons in that thing!" Sargon said. "We will be swept away like pooing sticks."

Courage was half way up the ladder. She stopped and gave them a cheery wave.

"She's certainly perked up." Arthur gestured back.

"False hope will unquestionably have that effect." Sargon felt his makeshift armour. "I am fervently wishing I had not watched the DVD of *Titanic*."

"I get the feeling you've gone through a lot in your life," Arthur said. "But I doubt you've ever actually been swept through a building on a homemade tidal wave."

"You are making a superb point." Sargon picked up the axe. "I will get prising."

By the time he had finished, Courage had returned.

"Cable's fixed to the rim at the top."

"Then you two get going and don't stop until the fire prevents you getting any further." Arthur wheeled over the davit. "I'll give you five minutes, then turn on the winch."

"I thought you were not interested in committing suicide." Sargon pulled him back. "It is I who should operate the thingamajig. Though my extremities are already jello at the thought, for I do not even like taking a bath."

"I can't move fast and I'm numb from the waist down." Arthur pointed out. "What difference will a few more knocks make?"

"It will make a difference if your head is knocked from your shoulders. You have the most first rate ideas of us all - and we will surely have more sticky wickets to bowl over."

"So we'll need your expertise with fires, won't we?"

"This is true."

They both turned and looked at Courage.

"I'm not offering," she said indignantly. "But I doubt Arthur can operate the winch, so it'll have to be you, Sargon."

"Of course I can operate it!" The boy bristled. "All you do is press the red button on the side. Why does everyone treat me like…"

"This one?" Courage leaned forwards and thumped the button. "Yeah. It *is* easy."

The cable went taut and a metallic rasp emanated from the tower.

"Argument solved."

"Holy crap!" Arthur spun his chair round and wheeled for safety, Sargon wobbling along behind. Courage easily outpaced them and was waiting at the door.

"Up you get, Arthur." She knelt down and the boy threw his hands round her neck. As she struggled to her feet, Sargon passed them and began to hop down the stairs.

There was a metallic screech from the tower as the supporting legs began to buckle.

Courage jogged downwards, Arthur bobbing precariously on her back.

"Ladies first." She elbowed Sargon out of the way.

"We are like the Wacky Races on television," he puffed, trying to catch up. "Though I have not yet seen an episode where everybody dies before the finishing line."

There was another tortured squeal from the roof as they reached the 19th floor. Then the sound of the tower tipping.

The teens skirted the punctures in the floor, now spewing flames into the air.

"Down you go." Courage dumped Arthur unceremoniously on the ground once they were past the fiery gaps. "Grab something that's not my neck."

Arthur pulled himself to an open door and held onto the frame. The girl took the next opening and did the same.

Sargon stood in the middle of the corridor, arms held loosely by his side, shifting from foot to foot.

"What are you waiting for?" Courage yelled. "Get to something solid!"

"I am altering my horses in mid-stream," the teen said. "And must trust that fortune favours the bold."

His voice was drowned out by a loud hiss, rising to a deafening roar.

Arthur shut his eyes.

A foaming torrent burst out of the open stairwell and thundered towards them, while white walls of water cascaded through the skylight roofs, swirling into the management offices, demolishing desks and knocking chairs aside. Courage and Arthur sucked in as much air as their lungs could take and held their breaths.

Sargon hobbled silently towards the maelstrom. Just as they were about to collide, he sank to his knees and rolled into one of the burning fissures. The torrent followed him down, creating an instant whirlpool.

Arthur and Courage were hit by a freezing torrent that almost tore them loose from their meagre sanctuary. Arthur felt the helmet camera being whisked from his head and suddenly he was under water. The teens held on until their arms were burning, but the undertow sucked at them with a force they couldn't resist. A dislodged desk drawer slammed into the girl's shoulder and she vanished down the corridor, fighting to keep her head above the water.

Arthur didn't last much longer. His fingers were wrenched from the door frame and he flailed wildly, trying to reach the surface. His head banged against the roof and he sucked in another lungful of air before the swirling eddies forced him underwater again. An office chair shot past, upside down, narrowly missing the boy.

He crashed into the wall at the end of the corridor and felt himself descending the stairs at a dizzying pace. Down and down he went, revolving like a top, until he didn't know which way he was facing. The teen felt blackness creep over him and his upper body began to go as limp as his legs.

Now I know what real helplessness is like, he thought

A hand grabbed his hair and pulled. Arthur grasped the wrist it was attached to and was guided to a metal strut. He clung on for dear life until the cascade subsided.

"Still alive then?" Courage had both arms and legs wrapped around the stairwell railing. Auburn hair was plastered to her face, stained even redder by a gash on her forehead.

Arthur retched loudly and spewed out a mouthful of dirty water.

"That was intense!" he spluttered. "Can we do it again?"

"No."

Suddenly, they were plunged into darkness. A few seconds later, red emergency lights flickered into life, turning the stairwell into a soggy version of Hades.

"I think we short-circuited the building," Courage coughed. "The backup generators must have finally kicked in."

"We have to go find Sargon!" Arthur finally let go and flopped onto the stairs. "What if he burned up?"

"Not with all that water right behind him." For the first time, there was a trace of admiration in the girl's voice. "He's annoying but not stupid."

"You're right," Arthur said sarcastically. "He probably just drowned."

"Chance would be a fine thing."

"He might be dead!" the teen gasped. "How could you *say* something so horrible?"

"Cause he's standing up there."

"Does anyone possess a blow dryer?" Sargon was leaning over the balcony railing a floor above them. "My magnificent quiff has gone flaccid as a pancake."

"Sargon!" Arthur whooped. "You're still with us!"

"Told you," Courage grunted.

"So it would seem." Sargon plodded down, his hobble more pronounced than before. "Though I now know exactly how a rubber duckie feels."

Like his companions, he was soaked to the skin and his cast was chipped and dented. He removed water wings from each arm and pushed up his goggles.

"On the plus side, the fire is most definitely extinguished."

20

Brandon Gollege had just finished his first stint on the anchor point. Mostly he had held a length of the hose firm, to stop it bucking, while more experienced men directed a stream of water at the fire. Then, for five minutes, they had let him take over the nozzle. It was the only way to learn properly, they said.

And they were right. He had easily weathered the heat, fumes, shouting and confusion in the mock fires he had tackled. The real thing was far more exhilarating. Terrifying too, but for a reason he hadn't expected.

It was the sense of responsibility. The feeling that lives depended on him keeping a clear head.

He silently thanked God the building was deserted and his companions were more skilled than he. If he made a mistake, they would correct it.

But it wouldn't always be that way. For the first time, he truly understood what it meant to be a firefighter. He silently vowed never to let down any of his future comrades or those in need of rescue. He would do whatever it took to protect and serve.

He was sitting by the cab, rubbing soot from his eyes, when Bailly marched over.

"Nice work, Puppy." He patted the boy's shoulder. "Stick around for a few minutes."

He indicated a car drawing up.

"You're about to get a deck at a living legend."

Deputy Chief Markham Silver unfolded himself from the driver's side like a spider emerging from its lair. Tall and impossibly thin for a man in his fifties, he strode over to Bailly's temporary command centre and gave the man a cursory salute. Pleasantries could come later.

"Thank you for briefing me over the radio," he said brusquely. "But I'd like a quick recap if you don't mind."

"We've got five trucks here now," Bailly said. "We're working fifteen minute shifts from an anchor point on the fourth floor. Brandon here just did his."

"And your progress report?"

Brandon blinked rapidly. The Deputy Chief was addressing *him*.

"It's my first fire," he stammered.

"Not what I asked."

The youth remembered his promise and cleared his throat.

"I think we can contain this portion," he said. "It's working its way upwards but so are we. Might take a couple of hours but we'll put it out, eventually."

Bailly nodded his approval and gave Brandon a thumbs up.

"Excellent," Markham said curtly. "We don't have high ladder, so I ordered a hundred footer platform from the Glasgow department to tackle the upper stories. Unfortunately, it will take well over an hour to arrive."

He glanced upwards.

"However, there seems to have been a new development."

The fire on the nineteenth floor was out and water was dripping from the blackened shells of several shattered windows.

"There was a water tower on the roof." Bailly followed his gaze. "Seems it fell over and the contents extinguished the blaze."

"Seems?" Markham picked up on the phrase immediately. "Either it did or it didn't."

"Obviously, the upper fire must have caused it to collapse. But... it didn't look like the blaze had reached the roof. It was two floors below."

"You know how sneaky conflagrations can be. Could have burnt right up the middle of the building. We wouldn't be able to tell from down here."

"That's true," Bailly admitted. "It just came down very... clean and fast."

"Out with it," Markham commanded. "You're a fine officer. If you have doubts, I want to hear them."

"One of the policemen in the main hospital was approached by a large nurse, who said two teenagers are unaccounted for."

That got his commander's attention.

"Give me the details."

"Apparently, they left a note saying they were going outside. Before everything kicked off. Now she can't find them."

"That should have been the first thing you told me," Markham reprimanded.

"I know. Sorry, Sir."

"So you're wondering if those strays might be trapped on the roof and pulled down the water tower." The Deputy Chief looked suitably sceptical. "That would be a pretty impressive endeavour for a couple of kids."

"Nearly impossible," Bailly agreed. "Especially since one is in a wheelchair and the other has his leg in a cast. The nurse said there was no way they could even get up there."

"But you're still worried."

"Until I can find them, yes. Stupid, I know. They're probably in the main hospital watching the whole she-bang from a window…"

Brandon coughed loudly.

"You have something to add?" Markham turned to him sharply

"I'm not far off being a kid myself," the rookie said sheepishly. "And I certainly wouldn't watch this from a distance. I'd come right back so I could see everything close up. Besides, wouldn't they want to know if their personal stuff had been saved?"

"Let's not take a chance then, eh?" Markham sounded impressed. "I'll call the coastguard and get a chopper to scope out the roof. I agree with Bailly that it's highly unlikely we'll find anyone there. Still, better to be safe than sorry."

He levelled a finger at Brandon.

"First encounter, eh, young man? Well done for speaking up. I'll be keeping an eye on you."

Brandon grinned from ear to ear.

21

"What were you thinking?" Arthur rounded on Sargon. "Jumping into that damned hole."

"I cannot swim," the boy replied. "Plus my cast is plaster and likely to soak up water."

He shook the soggy leg.

"This would quickly pull me to a watery grave, despite these feeble floatation devices, which were surely bought in Pound Stretcher."

"You didn't think to point that out before?" Arthur scolded.

"I felt you had plenty of vegetation on your plate already." Sargon apologised. "So I was depending that plenty water would get through the holes to put out the fire, but not enough to drown me."

"Dicey," Courage said. "But smart."

"Keep calm and try not to die, is my motto. I saw it on a mug."

"You could have broken your foot even worse."

"Which is why I landed on my butt. It is now feeling very raw."

"Hats off to you, Captain Hopeless," Arthur whistled. "A stunt like that took a giant pair of...."

"…Water wings." Courage pulled Arthur into a sitting position. "You two continue your love fest. I'm going to look downstairs."

"Jeez. Don't you want to take a breather?"

"It's breathing I'm worried about." Courage waved a hand around, stirring faint grey eddies in the air. "The fire is out, so where's this smoke coming from?

"You are like my Aunt Bashat. Always finding something new to fret over." Sargon pulled off his jumper. "She went to the hospital because she was sure her cough was the beginning of tuberculosis."

"And was it?"

"No. But the hospital was hit by a missile. All that was left were her false teeth."

Sargon removed his t-shirt and began to wring it out. Courage gave a start.

The boy's back was creased and puckered, covered from neck to waist in ugly white scars.

"As I mentioned before," he said, spotting her discomfort. "I know a lot about fires."

"Stay here." The girl put her goggles back on and began to descend the stairs. "Back soon."

Sargon waited until she was gone.

"Why is she still risking her life to help us?" he asked. "We are like dead weights around her neck. Only we are still alive, of course."

The boy had gotten all the moisture he could out of his top and quickly put it back on.

"After all, we stole her money and are the reason she is trapped."

"That was accidental." Arthur struggled out of his own t-shirt and squeezed it until the stream of muddy water turned to a trickle. "Maybe she's just a really good person."

"She is less friendly than Genghis Khan with a headache."

"That may be." Arthur pulled his clothing back on. "But she's certainly coming in handy."

"Talking of handy. Have you seen my axe? It is like Thor's hammer to me."

"Buried in the wall behind you." Arthur pointed. "Just missed my head at one point."

He looked around.

"Sargon? Why *is* the smoke getting thicker?"

"Because heat rises." The boy pulled his axe from the wall and leaned on it. "The ceilings on each level are a fine barrier to this. But the stairwell is open all the way down to the ground and acting like a funnel."

"Even so, it must be a hell of a blaze for the smoke to reach this height."

"I fear it is a doozy. And, unfortunately, there are no windows in the stairwells we can break to disperse the fumes."

He hefted the axe disconsolately.

"Most people die from smoke inhalation rather than burning. So we must stay near the ground whenever possible."

132 · Burnt Out

"Not really a problem for me." Arthur snapped the swimming goggles over his eyes. He crawled to the edge of the stairs and began to slide down, head first.

"What are you up to now, lunatic?"

"Can't let Courage have all the fun, eh?" Arthur was wriggling his way down the steps. "You with me?"

"Most certainly. I have not enjoyed myself so much since the last time I went on fire."

Sargon sat next to the boy and bumped his way down, holding onto Arthur's belt and using the axe as a punt.

"Floor seventeen," Arthur announced when they reached the next landing. "Sorry if this isn't very dig-nified to watch."

"You are not the one using your buttocks as a method of conveyance."

But the haze was getting thicker, irritating the boys' lungs. By the time they reached the 16th floor, both had begun to gag.

Half way down the next flight they encountered Courage. She was carrying three small metal bottles with plastic attachments.

"You mistake *stay there* for *follow me*?" she rasped. "Put these on."

She fastened a portable oxygen mask to Arthur's mouth with an elastic strap and he breathed deeply. She clasped the second to her face and handed the third to Sargon.

"We will have to work out a method of hand signals if we are wearing these," the boy said.

"Easily done." Courage raised a middle finger. "Figure this one out?"

"I am getting the message loud and clearly." Sargon put on the mask. "You are impervious to my considerable charms."

"Yeah," Arthur asked in a muffled voice. "What have you got against Sargon?"

"Never been a people person." Courage began to descend again. "Not too fond of you either, if it helps."

"You were right," Sargon nudged Arthur. "She is a regular Saint Joan of Ark."

"Even brought her own fire," the boy giggled, fogging his mask even more.

"Come ON," Courage growled.

They descended another four flights to level twelve, the girl holding Arthur's bottle while he crawled. There was no sound except for their ragged exhalations, for everything else was muffled by the fug of smoke. The stairwell was so thick with noxious fumes they could hardly see.

Arthur began to choke, thumping his chest violently. Courage was finding it hard to catch her breath too. She shook the oxygen bottle and motioned to the fire door. She and Sargon opened it, pulled Arthur into the corridor and quickly shut it again.

The air was much clearer here and they removed the masks.

"Stupid bottles were nearly empty," the girl groaned. "Nothing in this fucking place works the way it should."

"We can't get any further down the stairs," Arthur said dolefully. "Will we try the ones at the other end? See if they're clearer."

"May as well." Courage agreed. "There's a bunch of big oxygen tanks stored in a cupboard on this floor. Let's hope there's some more portable ones in there too."

"Is that not against hospital rules?" Sargon asked. "I read in a manual that such hazards should be kept a safe distance from any main buildings."

"You know your stuff," Courage acknowledged. "But since Eden Heights is getting demolished soon, the orderlies figured it was no big deal."

"You're more than familiar with this building," Arthur remarked. "You seem to know exactly how the place operates and where every little thing is."

"I'm observant," the girl snapped. "You complaining?"

"I just think it's weird."

"Bicker not, comrades." Sargon pointed. "Look. Arthur has a new chariot."

In the empty corridor was another wheelchair.

"I believe luck is finally being a lady tonight," he grinned. "That is a Frank Sinatra song I am most fond of. Unfortunately, singers in my country sound like they are gargling tea."

"Here you go." Courage helped Arthur into the seat.

"It's a lot nicer than my last one." Arthur spun in a circle. "Very smooth and sexy."

"A bit like myself." Sargon clumped off down the passageway, leaning on his axe. "Do not be tardy, peeps. I am keen to see which form our next brush with death will take."

"The oxygen tanks are in here." Courage stopped at a door.

"Let us try the other stairs first," Sargon suggested. "Those bottles are very flammable and I would be more comfortable if I did not have a potential bomb strapped to my face."

"I so want to make a terrorist joke right now," Arthur deadpanned.

"Please refrain from such childishness," Sargon sniffed back. "I will have most definitely heard it before."

"Can the double act, guys," Courage hurried them along. "Or, I swear I'll leave you behind."

They eventually reached the far end of the hospital and she looked through the window of the fire door. It was also crisscrossed with wire and impossible to shatter.

"Can't see any smoke."

She tried to turn the handle but it wouldn't budge.

"You bloody joking?" She twisted harder. "It's locked!"

"*Why?*"

"Because nobody is supposed to be up here unless they have a key."

"Never fear, agitated chums." Sargon lifted the axe. "I am rather the expert at getting out of tricky situations."

"No, it's reinforced and…"

Before Courage could finish, Sargon brought the blade crashing down on the handle. It sheared off and bounced along the corridor.

"…And the lock is inside this." Courage knocked on a metal plate. "Now we really can't get it open."

"My apologies."

"You're a dumbass."

"Hey! Arguing won't help anyone," Arthur broke in. "We'll stick to plan A."

"We *have* a plan?"

"We do," Arthur insisted. "Get the portable oxygen bottles and go down the other stairs to the next level. If we can't see, we'll just have to feel our way."

"Told you." Courage strode off, the boys trying to keep pace. As the girl reached the cupboard, Sargon went over on his ankle and gave a cry of pain. He reached out and placed a hand on the wall to steady himself.

"OMFG!"

He pushed himself upright and sprinted towards Courage, ignoring the searing pain in his leg.

"Wait!" he screamed. "The wall is hot!"

He was too late. The girl turned the handle and pushed.

Sargon clenched his fists, put all the weight he could on his good leg, then leapt. He slammed into Courage, knocking her sideways.

Air was sucked into the cupboard and a giant spiral of fire billowed out. It ignited the opposite wall, then raced along the roof towards Arthur.

22

Courage was on her feet in a second. She scooped up Sargon and threw his arm round her neck. Then they raced towards Arthur, both bent low to avoid the conflagration devouring the ceiling. The boy was already wheeling backwards to get away from the heat. He spun round in one fluid motion and continued onwards.

"Where is the largest ward?" Sargon shouted. "One that has a bathroom."

"We have to fight our way back!" Courage let him go and pulled a fire extinguisher from the wall. "Otherwise, we're cut off from the only open stairwell."

There was now a barrier of shimmering orange filling the corridor. The walls were blistering and gobbets of flaming polystyrene dripped from the roof.

"No time!" Sargon grabbed the girl by her shoulder. "We are needing a big ward, I tell you. One with showers and a bath. Where?"

"Next to the locked stairwell," Courage relented. "You better be right about this."

Arthur was already whizzing towards it, arms pumping the wheels of his chair.

They dashed to the end of the corridor and into the last room on the left, Courage slamming the door behind them. They found themselves in a large white ward full of abandoned beds.

"This will do nicely." Sargon glanced around approvingly.

"What are you sounding so pleased about?" Courage glanced at him testily. "We're trapped."

"The oxygen tanks are metal but they will rupture once the temperature gets too high." The teen began pulling a mattress from the nearest bed and dragging the bulky square awkwardly up the ward, flinching with each step. "There was not enough air in the cupboard for the fire to do more than smoulder until you opened the door and let it in. Now the tanks will surely explode."

"Oh." Courage sounded suitably chastised. "Better not be in the corridor when that happens."

"Exactly. Pull the mattresses to the bathroom at the far end," Sargon commanded. "As many as you can."

"Mattresses burn," Courage began. "Shouldn't...."

"Will you be having some confidence in me, woman?" The boy wheezed, winded by the exertion. "Arthur? Get into the bathroom and turn on the taps and showers. Put plugs in all the sinks and find a bath."

"I wouldn't mind soaking in a tub." Arthur wheeled off to the far end of the ward and vanished into the bathroom.

"I do admire that fellow," Sargon paused for a second to catch his breath. "He is most unflappable."

Courage helped him jostle five or six mattresses to the bathroom door and began to pull them through.

"Turned everything on," Arthur said wickedly. "The sinks are already overflowing and I didn't even put towels on the floor."

"Then help Courage pile these mattresses against the door."

Sargon looked around and spotted an old-fashioned bath, large and ceramic, with ornately shaped legs. He brought the axe down on the plumbing several times until he had sheared it in two.

"We must turn this over and get inside."

"All three of us?"

"I am not suggesting you include the wheelchair. But, yes."

Sargon and Courage tipped over the bath and held it up while Arthur manoeuvred himself out of the chair and rolled under. They slid in beside him and lowered the bath to the ground.

Blackness enveloped them.

"Someone's elbow is up my nose," Arthur complained.

"That's me." Courage squirmed around and her hand brushed Sargon's wet cheek.

"Your leg must be in agony after all this," she whispered. "I'm sorry."

"It is tap water, not tears," the boy replied defensively. "Though I admit, I am sore in my heart."

"Why?"

"I do not like explosions. But that is a conversation for another time."

"What about you Arthur?"

"I have mixed feelings," the boy said calmly. "I never thought anything thrilling would happen to me again. And now that it has, I'm elated and petrified at the same time."

He gave a short laugh.

"I was fed up of living and now I'm scared of dying. Does that sound strange?"

Courage reached out in the dark and took both their hands.

"Everything about this situation is strange," she said.

Her voice was drowned out as the oxygen tanks exploded.

The building shook and a deafening roar filled their ears. The bath was pushed across the floor and slammed against the far wall. The teens clutched at their throats, for all the air seemed to have been pulled from around them. Pieces of ceiling rained down on the upturned porcelain, rattling like a staccato drum. The water lapping around the trio suddenly drained away.

Then ominous silence.

"Still hate taking a bath, Sargon?" Arthur asked.

"I am vastly preferring it this way up."

"Now we'll have the blaze to contend with." Courage arched her back and cautiously lifted their cover. "Whole place must be an inferno."

"I do not think so." Sargon crawled out. "A big explosion will burn up all the neighbouring oxygen in seconds and the shockwave will blow out the remaining flames. We should be safe for a while."

They tipped the bath upright and freed Arthur. The atmosphere was stifling and their surroundings seared black, but there was no sign of any fire.

"We've now put out two major conflagrations," the boy said gleefully. "I see a career in emergency services beckoning."

"I would certainly look splendid in a bright red uniform and shiny boots." Sargon mused.

"That's the Canadian Mounties. But you'd have your very own axe. I know how much you like it."

"Indeed. I am glad it did not end up buried in your head."

"Me too."

"In fact, I am thinking of giving it a name. What about Choppy McChopface?"

"Now you sound like a serial killer."

"My God." Courage groaned. "You two deserve to die."

The tiles of the shower room were a myriad of spidery cracks and the wall adjoining the ward was buckled, plaster broken off in lumps. The mattresses buttressing the door were tattered and smoking and most had been blown over.

The girl got up, pulled them aside and peered carefully out of the ruined frame.

"Good news," she said. "Sargon's right. The fire is gone."

There was a small cheer from behind her.

"Bad news? So is the floor."

"What?" Sargon shuffled over.

"In fact, a few levels seem to have vanished."

23

Fire-fighters scattered as a huge section of the Eye-sore above them burst outward, a concrete bubble wrapped in its own lambent halo. A sonic boom rent the air. Men and women dived for the ground or scrambled under trucks, as falling masonry, flying glass and metal rained down.

After a few seconds, the noise faded away. Ash floated through the air and settled on the bodies slowly rising to their feet.

Bailly pulled himself upright, ears ringing, and grabbed the radio.

"Anchor point. What's your status?"

Same as before, a voice crackled back. *What the hell was that sound?*

The man leaned against his truck, overcome with relief.

"An explosion several floors above you."

We're fine and the hoses are still flowing. Don't worry about us. Do what you have to do out there.

"All units. I want to know if anyone was hurt." Bailly could see a group of doctors and nurses running towards the scene, some carrying stretchers. "Report back to me immediately."

He waved his arms at the medical staff.

"Stay away!" he yelled. "It's too dangerous!"

"This is *our* job," a nurse with a badge saying *Doreen Jones* shouted back. "We'll take your casualties to the main hospital. It's the least we can do."

She put her hands on large hips, daring him to object.

Bailly didn't.

A few minutes later, Markham Silver marched over. His helmet was askew and a large cut snaked down one arm under his torn tunic. Despite the wound, he seemed unruffled. He always did.

"Are my men all right?"

"A couple of broken bones and some minor lacerations." Bailly looked up from his radio. "They're being moved to the main hospital by staff. All things considered, we got lucky."

"I'd say so." The Deputy Chief looked up at a gaping hole fourteen stories above. "The force of the blast seems to have extinguished any fires on that level."

"And the anchor point is still holding."

Markham surveyed the debris.

"The chopper is only minutes away but that gale is turning into a full blown tempest."

"Yeah, and still no rain."

"Unfortunately, it's not that kind of storm. The pilot is reporting gusts of up to sixty knots, constantly changing direction, and he's having trouble staying aloft. Which means the high platform, when it arrives, will be useless. Fully extended, it would get blown around like a twig."

He gave a weary sigh.

"I'd like to get my hands on whoever approved constructing a multi-storey on top of an unprotected hill."

Bailly cupped his ear. Both men could now hear the faint sound of a rotor.

"I've asked him to land so we can put a man on board," Markham said. "It's a coastguard chopper and they're great at pulling people out of rough seas. But this isn't their area of expertise."

He hesitated.

"Giving how dangerous it might be, I'll have to call on a volunteer."

"I'm happy to go," Bailly said. "Well… happy is probably the wrong word."

"Not an option. I need you here to help coordinate operations."

"Then I'm your man." Brandon rounded the side of the truck, followed by Tyres.

"Sorry, Puppy." Bailly waved him away. "Need someone with a bit more know-how."

"No offence son," Markham added. "But I have grandchildren older than you."

"Of course." Brandon looked crestfallen. "Just thought I'd ask."

"Looks like it's me then." Tyres stepped forward. "I like operating things. Think he'll give me go at the controls?"

As if on cue, the blunt outline of a MH-65 Dolphin hove into view. It dipped alarmingly, then righted, descended and settled onto the grass fifty yards away.

Tyres swallowed hard.

"Sally Hampton here is one of my finest, despite her driving." Bailly introduced the woman. "She's been showing Brandon the ropes."

"Honoured to meet you." Markham shook her hand. "Though I can feel you're trembling a bit. Afraid of flying by any chance?"

"I… eh… like vehicles with four wheels better."

"Have you ever actually been in a chopper before?"

"No, Sir."

The Deputy Chief tapped thin fingers together.

"Tell you what. Take your protégé with you. I want him to learn from the best."

"Really?" Brandon goggled. "Are you serious?"

"I'm always serious. And please address me as Sir. It's protocol."

"Yes Sir!" The pair saluted. "We won't let you down."

Bailly smiled to himself. His superior had just massively breached protocol himself by giving Tyres the rookie to look after. But he understood why.

The Deputy Chief was well aware she wouldn't want to lose face in front of someone who so obviously admired her. She'd cope with whatever the elements threw at her now.

That's why Markham Silver was a legend.

24

Sargon leaned over the precipice. The force of the blast had caused the whole ward to collapse on itself. The contents had crashed into the next level, followed by the shockwave, demolishing the floor below. The weight had created a domino effect, taking out the next three levels. They could see all the way to the tenth floor, through a tangle of rubble, steel girders, and jagged metal cables, intermingled with mangled beds, broken slabs of concrete and dripping pipes. The carnage stretched from wall to wall, leaving only a narrow rim, no wider than a windowsill.

While Sargon and Courage gaped, Arthur managed to right his wheelchair and pull himself into the seat.

"At least my trusty steed is still working." He wheeled over to his companions. "Holy Mother of God!"

"Big, isn't it?" Courage said morosely.

"Can you climb down?"

"We do not know how secure the rubble is," Sargon pointed out. "Courage might cause the whole thing to slide if she stands on it."

"You saying I need to go on a diet?"

"I can never tell if you are joking." The boy raised an eyebrow. "You are an exceedingly queer fish."

"At least you're not calling me a whale."

"*Could* you work your way along the ledge next to the wall?" Arthur asked. "I'd do it but...." He patted the chair. "Never thought I'd be glad to get kept from the action."

"I can try," Courage said. "What about you two?"

"You might find a rope or something. Throw it to us." He pointed to a massive gap in the outer wall on the other side of the ward. "Or maybe you'll be able to signal for attention. The explosion knocked a hole right through to the outside."

"All right." There was a tremor in the girl's voice. "Looks a bit dangerous, though."

"Looks like certain death, if you are asking me," Sargon replied vehemently. "You should most definitely not attempt this."

"Now I've got to go. Can't be seen agreeing with anything this one says."

She winked at Sargon.

"Thank you for saving my life, though. Again."

"You are most welcome, grumpy pants."

"My turn to be a champion, I guess." Courage pressed her back and hands against the wall and began to inch along the ledge. Two feet. Then five. Then ten.

She gave a tentative smile.

"Aw, this is too easy..."

As she spoke, the ledge collapsed.

Courage dropped, twisting in mid-air. She threw up her hands, grabbed the remains of the outcrop and clung on, feet scrabbling for purchase. Arthur covered his eyes.

The girl hung, suspended, for a few seconds. Then she placed both knees against the broken brickwork below and hefted herself up. Got her elbows back on the ledge.

"You can do it!" Sargon shouted. "Do not freak out!"

Courage swung one leg onto the parapet, but the rim was too narrow and it slid back off. She tried again, with no more success.

"I can't," she said. "Don't have the strength."

"Just you hold on," Sargon looked around. "I am coming."

"You'll never make it. Not in that cast."

"I fear you are right." The boy grabbed the axe and swallowed hard.

He swung it above his head and brought the back of the blade down on his calf. The cast split in two.

"Ow, ow, ow!"

"Are you nuts?" Arthur gasped.

"You are not the first to question my mental state." Sargon bent over and peeled off the broken plaster, white patches sticking to his shin. He stood up and gingerly put weight on the limb.

"Stiff and sore. But I shall never have to shave my leg again. Not that I do, of course."

He stepped onto the ledge and worked his way along, face set in a pained scowl.

"Please hurry," Arthur urged. "She's slipping."

Sargon reached Courage as the last of her strength drained away.

"Can't hold on," she whispered.

"Grab my hand."

"I'm too heavy. I'll tip you over."

As her elbow slipped from the rim, Sargon reached down and seized the girl's wrist.

"Gggggggggggrgh!"

He straightened up, Courage dangling over the void below him. Sinews stood out on the boy's arms and neck as he pulled. The girl's feet windmilled until they found the ledge and she pressed herself against the wall, sobbing quietly.

"Forget about the mounted police," Sargon wheezed. "Management will most likely hire me to re-place the broken winch on the roof."

The pair scuffled back to safety and Arthur helped them, as best he could, to solid ground.

Courage crouched down, taking small, quick breaths. Sargon sat beside her, massaging his calf.

"You all right?" Arthur asked.

"This annoyance was due to come off soon, any-way." The boy shrugged. "I just speeded up the process."

"What an incredibly stupid thing to do." Courage leaned over and kissed him on the cheek. "You're the most irritating person I ever met."

"I shall consider myself chastised," he beamed.

The girl lay back and stared at the blackened ceiling.

"So, do we have another escape route?"

"I don't think we have a choice." Arthur rubbed his hands together apprehensively.

"We'll have to go into that hole."

-Part 3-

The Descent

> *If you want to go fast, go alone. If you want to go far, go together.*
>
> African Proverb

25

"It's like Hades down there," Courage shuddered. "Who's going first?"

"We're taking a breather," Arthur said. "And thinking things through before we do anything rash."

"We'd never want to do anything rash, eh?"

"There's a first aid cabinet on the floor over there, Courage. Can you bandage Sargon's ankle?"

"I'll try." The girl fetched a roll of gauze and scissors from the broken metal box and began to wrap it around her companion's foot. "But I'm not a real nurse, remember?"

"That's all right," Arthur said cryptically. "Sargon isn't what he seems either."

They both stared at him.

"You are sprouting seven kinds of nonsense and perhaps eight." Sargon stammered. "Am I looking like Joseph Bloggs from number 10 next door?"

"You've memorised more English words than I'll ever learn, plus you know exactly how to use them." Arthur shook his head. "The clumsy mistakes you make every now and then are deliberate and I've figured out why."

"Do tell."

"To make you seem bumbling and harmless."

"There is no need to be insulting…"

"But your tolerance for pain is off the charts," Arthur continued. "So is your stamina. I've been working out for years and I couldn't have lifted Courage like that."

"Don't *you* start on my weight." The girl snipped off the end of the gauze and tied it in a knot.

"You have burns all over your back but still don't shy away from fire. No normal person is that tough."

"I am Captain Hopeless." Sargon gave a cheesy grin. "This is what we superheroes are like."

"Superhero is a pretty accurate description. You're in here because you wiped the floor with four Niddrie hard men. I overheard the staff gossiping about it."

"I got in a couple of lucky punches." Sargon dropped the act and glared at him coldly. "What of it?"

"You put them all in hospital," Arthur insisted. "You've been trained for combat."

"Leave him alone," Courage interrupted. "It's none of our damned business."

"I must agree with the lady," Sargon said menacingly, his amiable mask slipping further. "My past is none of your affair."

But Arthur wasn't the type to be intimidated.

"You misunderstand." He didn't look away. "I don't care what you used to be before we met and neither does Courage."

He laid a hand on his friend's shoulder.

"So stop risking your life to prove you're one of the good guys."

"I am awkward with sentiments, so allow me to keep a zip on my stiff upper lip," Sargon muttered. "You are more perceptive than I was realising."

"Enough to know you're not going to follow my advice."

"Then let us proceed without further discussion." Sargon smoothly switched topics. "We have been lazing around like Greek taxi drivers."

"That rubble might still give way." Courage stood up. "I better go first."

"I think not." Sargon pulled her back. "Burnt-out buildings are familiar territory to me, so I shall venture into the pit."

"Arthur was right," Courage sighed. "You're determined to get yourself killed. Well, I can play the…"

"Let's get something straight," Arthur broke in. "I thought we agreed *I'm* in charge of planning."

"You are."

"Then *I'm* going."

"Arthur." Sargon twiddled his thumbs awkwardly. "Your bravery is not in dispute but you are not exactly… agile."

"He means you'll never get down there." Courage tested the lip of the crevasse with her foot. "If that scree is unstable and collapses, you can't even jump out of the way."

"Which is why we're going to push the bath over first, to test it."

"Now you are cooking with gas," Sargon said approvingly. "Though that is perhaps an inappropriate metaphor."

"And I intend to be inside," Arthur continued.

"And this is *also* a terrible plan. You are close to being demoted."

"As you guys helpfully pointed out," the boy replied indignantly. "How else am I going to get down? Besides, I've still got my protective gear on."

"You will surely topple out and the damned thing will land on you. Is *killed by a falling bath* really what you desire on your tombstone?"

"Put a mattress over the top and tie it in place with the rest of the bandages. I'll be like a turtle in its shell. Might even have a snooze while I'm waiting."

"An eternal snooze," Courage said. "Forget it."

"I'm not asking. I'm telling. Stop trying to hog all the glory."

"Unfortunately, Arthur is right." Sargon stood. "It is his best chance and we do not have time to argue."

Courage and Sargon stood by the bath, which had been manoeuvred to the edge of the precipice. They had put the thickest and least damaged mattress on top and secured it with long strips of gauze.

"You ready, daredevil?" Courage asked.

"Can't hear too well." The boy's voice was barely audible. "Are we there yet?"

"On the count of three." She and Sargon placed their hands on the porcelain side. "One... two... go!"

Both shoved and the bath slid over the edge. It skied down a few feet, hit a girder and flipped upside down.

"Jesus!" Courage turned away. "No, no!"

The bath continued down, tumbling over and over, gathering momentum. Pipes and cables pierced the mattress, sending spouts of foam into the air. Chunks of concrete were pulverised by the improvised missile and one of the ornate legs flew off.

"Oh, Arthur." Sargon followed the trajectory, transfixed. "This is a dreadful sight to behold."

The bath reached the bottom of the incline, finally righting itself, the covering tattered and pierced. A mushroom of fine dust drifted lazily upwards.

"You think he's all right?" Courage finally took her hands from her face.

"I am not a betting man. But, if I were, I would always put my money on Mr Indestructible."

There was a loud creaking and the bath suddenly disappeared, leaving a puff of grey powder. Where it had been was now a dark fissure.

"I believe the odds have changed."

"He's fallen through to the floor below." Courage started forwards.

"I know you will want to rush and get to our friend as quickly as possible." Sargon held the girl back.

"This you must not do. Be measured and steady and test every hand and foothold before you put your full weight on it."

"I will."

Courage began to climb down. The going was slow but not difficult, for the terrain was rugged and there were plenty of protuberances to hold.

"This is easier than I thought." She glanced around for her companion.

"Sargon?"

The boy was already half way down the slope, despite his injury, shimmying between slabs and girders like a mountaineer. The ever-present axe in his hand only added to the illusion.

"Hey! What happened to measured and steady?"

"Those were instructions for you. I never listen to myself."

"You're a moron."

The further Courage descended, the faster she was able to go. The scree was sheer at the top but curved as it went down, like a narrowing funnel. By the time she reached the bottom, Sargon was lying on his stomach peering into the hole and shouting Arthur's name.

Courage joined him. The bath stood upright in the corridor below, a huge crack down one side, looking horribly like a white coffin.

"Any answer?"

"Not a peep." Sargon shuffled around and hung off the edge. "I am going down."

The boy let go, swinging his legs up. He landed spread-eagled on the mattress, sending up a cloud of dirt, then rolled off onto the floor.

"Nice move." Courage jumped down too, pulled the scissors from her pocket and began to attack the bandages. Once they were gone, the pair pulled away the mattress.

Arthur lay curled in a ball, limp and unresponsive.

They gently pulled him out and laid the boy on the floor.

"Is he breathing?" Courage felt his chest. "I don't know if he's breathing."

"You must perform CGI on him," Sargon demanded.

"It's CPR," Courage said. "And, for the last time, I'm not a real nurse."

"That's all right." Arthur opened his eyes and grinned. "I'm not a real casualty. Could do with some Aspirin though."

26

The Dolphin rose up the side of Eden Heights, buffeted by arctic blasts. It dipped and bucked as the pilot fought to keep his bird under control. Brandon gripped the arm rests until his knuckles ached. Next to him, the winch man yawned loudly and settled down in his seat.

"You get used to it," he said laconically.

They passed the giant hole in the building, a gaping dragon's mouth, ringed with broken girders and breathing out smoke.

No sign of anyone.

But their glimpse was momentary, for the sight was quickly enveloped in a monochrome fog. It swirled and snaked upwards, only to be dispersed when it reached the top, massing into a flat black haze scudding away over the hills.

A flash of lightning cut across the sky.

"Tell me what's happening here," Tyres said tensely from the back seat, trying to take her mind off their precarious situation.

"Heat from the fire is being sucked through the chasm into the cold air outside," Brandon replied. "It's causing massive invection currents and adding to the turbulence."

"Thanks for the heads-up." The pilot rose above the building, where crosswinds swung the chopper ninety degrees. He pulled sideways on the joystick and the helicopter reared like a frightened colt. "Be quick. I can't hold this position long."

Brandon began taking pictures of the roof on his mobile while Tyres reported back on the walkie-talkie.

"Half the roof is covered in tied-down tarpaulin," she said. "The other section has scaffolding, debris and what's left of the water tower scattered around. I can't see any signs of life."

"Good job. There's no way I could land on that terrain." The pilot risked a quick look and the chopper shot down several feet.

"If you lowered me, it wouldn't do any good," the winch man added. "I'd be blown around like fluff in a vacuum cleaner. Never be able to pick anyone up."

"In fact, if I don't get out of here right now, we're going to end up on that roof, after all," the pilot said. "In pieces."

As if to confirm his fears, the Dolphin shot sideways and revolved again. Tyres gave a small squeak.

"I'm cool with landing." She reached out and grabbed Brandon's hand. "Right now. Now is fine. You agree, Puppy?"

"Most definitely." Brandon had turned green. "I thought our job was dangerous. Thank God I didn't join the Coast Guard, even if you got cooler helmets."

He stared at the pilot and winch man.

"They ought to give you bloody medals every time you get into this thing."

Once they had landed, Tyres and Brandon shakily made their way to the control centre, where Bailly and Markham were waiting.

"There's no sign of the fire having reached the roof but we couldn't see any people either." Brandon showed them the pictures on his mobile. "Pilot says it's impossible to land any of our men to check, not that he could affect a rescue if we found survivors. It's like flying through the inside of a tumble dryer."

"Has anyone been spotted in the windows?" Markham asked Bailly.

"No. But, apparently, they're too dirty to see through and don't open. You can't even break them."

"Nevertheless, there's still no evidence of anyone in the building," Markham said. "What's your opinion?"

"The anchor point is holding though the men aren't making much headway," Bailly replied. "We can't direct water from the outside either, since most of the ladders were damaged by falling concrete. No way we can get past the fire to search the upper floors."

"Couldn't we switch on the service elevator?" Brandon suggested. "It's in the basement and looks pretty sturdy."

"It was built before safety overrides were invented," the station commander replied. "Which means any fire will activate the call button on the affected landing, causing the lift to stop there. You'd be incinerated before you could close the door again."

"In other words, not a chance."

"Do we know what caused the explosion yet?" Tyres asked.

"I was approached by one of the orderlies treating our men." Bailly massaged his temples. "He says staff have been storing oxygen tanks on the upper floors of this monstrosity rather than lugging them all the way to the perimeter sheds and back."

"That was pretty stupid."

"Stupid but understandable. There's only a couple of weeks to go before the building is due to be demolished, so they didn't consider it much of a risk."

"They were wrong," Markham said. "I'll wager that's what caused the latest explosion. Add the fact that there are any number of potential small files burning in empty wards and we're looking at a powder keg."

"Should I order a withdrawal?" Bailly had the radio poised in his hand.

"Hell, no. I don't give up that easy." The Deputy Chief took off his helmet and looked at it as if trying to gain strength from the authority it conveyed.

"It seems fairly safe to assume the Eyesore is deserted after all. And it better be. One more detonation and, despite our best efforts, this building is doomed."

He looked lost for a moment. Then he turned to Brandon and Tyres.

"You pair must be pretty shaken up after that ordeal."

"We're good to go, Sir," they replied in unison.

"Nevertheless, you've both earned a rest. Get back to the lower basement and keep an eye on things."

"Surely we can be more use up here?"

"You think that's not an important job?" Markham scowled. "If a blaze breaks out underneath our men and nobody notices, they'll be lucky to get out alive."

"We're on it."

27

Courage cradled Arthur's head on her lap while he recovered.

"Which floor are we on now?" he asked groggily. "I've lost count."

"Ninth." Courage said. "Sargon is going from ward to ward, breaking the few panes he can with his axe. Guy should have been a lumberjack. Or a mass murderer."

They could hear glass cracking in the distance. Slowly the dirty air began to disperse, as the freezing air outside sucked fumes away.

"Let's be moving on then." Arthur tried to sit up. "I get bored easily."

"Take a rest." The girl pushed him back down. "You've just had seven bells knocked out of you."

"Wasn't going to sprint. You'll have to carry me until we find another wheelchair."

"Then *I'm* taking a break. There's no sign of any fire at the moment."

"Which means I have time to ask." Arthur looked up at her quizzically. "Why did you run away from home?"

"No big mystery," Courage sighed. "My mum's an alcoholic waste of space."

"And your dad?"

"My dad will be looking for me, all right. In fact, he'll never stop." The girl looked quickly away. "Can't *ever* let that violent bastard find me."

"Maybe you should tell Sargon. He's not a guy to cross and I can tell you two have a thing for each other."

"Don't be so daft." She punched the boy's shoulder. "And keep your voice down. Here he comes."

"The atmosphere is now more cordial, though I could not break more than a few panes." Sargon returned, axe over his shoulder. "When I opened the fire door, however, the stairwell was another matter. It has more smoke than a heavy metal concert."

"Didn't think you'd ever been to a heavy metal concert."

"It is on my bucket list. So I am thinking I have about half an hour to see one."

"That bad?"

"There is an unpleasant glow further down the stairs and the heat rising is intense. The floors between us and any fire-fighters must be an inferno."

"You mean we have to go back the way we came?" Arthur stared at the mangled slope. "After all the effort it took to get here?"

"I would caution against that." Sargon sat down heavily. "Flames are licking up the outside and going up will take much longer than coming down. The fire would overtake us long before we reach the roof."

He opened the nearest door. Through the filthy window panes they could make out a sickly flickering luminescence, dancing behind opaque glass.

"I thought that was flashing lights from the emergency vehicles," Courage said quietly.

"I tried to attract attention again," Sargon continued. "But the lights are too dim and the building is wrapped in a blanket of smoke. It is no use."

"What about the glass you've been shattering?"

"Everyone will think heat is to blame. This is normal."

"How long would it take to prise a whole frame loose with your axe?"

"Longer than we have. Besides, we are still too high for any ladder to reach."

"You could get back to the roof a lot faster without me," Arthur suggested hesitantly.

"Not quickly enough. And where would we go from there?" Courage felt the floor. "It's getting warmer."

"I know." Sargon seemed utterly defeated. "I fear we are finally trapped."

"Hey! None of that." Arthur clapped his hands. "We're not dead yet. Let's explore the options."

He ticked his fingers.

"We can't go up. We can't use the stairs. Could we tie blankets together to get past the burning floors?"

"Becoming human candles is not a course I favour." Sargon lay back with a groan. "Nor am I good with knots."

"What about the garbage and laundry chutes?"

"Too small for anyone to get into," Courage said. "Besides, they're probably on fire by now."

She drew up her knees and clasped them

"There's nowhere for us to go."

"I'm sorry we got you into this," Arthur said. "I really am."

"No. I'm the one who's sorry," Courage whispered. "This is all *my* fault."

"What do you mean?"

"I was rummaging in the bins a few weeks ago when the old janitor, Grant Coull, came across me."

"Is this a long tale?" Sargon asked. "We are a little pressed for time."

"I don't want to die without coming clean. It's important."

"There's nowhere to run, Sargon," Arthur reminded him. "We're trapped."

"Grant Coull asked why I was there," the girl continued. "So I told him everything. He gave me something to eat and said I could sleep in his basement office whenever he left for the night. Gave me a key and a nurse's uniform to make it easier for me to move around the hospital without getting caught."

"So that's why you know the place inside out," Arthur said. "You live here."

"A real gentleman, he was." Courage sniffed. "Know how I repaid him? I began to steal money from handbags and coats. Kept the cash in an urn at the back of a cupboard on the fifth floor. I was trying to save enough to get as far away from my dad as possible."

"This is indeed a pitiful tale," Sargon said. "But I still do not see how you caused all this."

"When he retired, Grant said I could still use his basement room cause the new janitor was busy with the main building and hardly ever came round to check. But the fuses in the boiler room were ancient and kept blowing."

The girl was a picture of misery.

"I didn't want anyone investigating and finding my hiding place but I had no idea how to replace fuse wire properly. So I used nails."

"Which would never blow," Arthur nodded. "Instead, any power surge would overload the wiring and start a fire."

"You are not an electrician," Sargon said weakly. "You were not to know."

"I'm not stupid either," the girl replied sadly. "I should have realised something bad could happen."

She gave a harsh laugh.

"This was supposed to be my last day in Eden Heights. I was on the way to get my money when I bumped into a cleaner who told me you were on the roof with an urn. I checked the cupboard where I hid the cash, but it was gone. So I started upstairs to get it back and there was an explosion below me."

"Yeah," Arthur grunted. "We heard."

"I thought I could still get the urn and rescue you too. That kinda backfired though." She patted the wad of notes, still safe inside her pocket. "Even if I live, I'd be put in jail for what I've done or handed back to my dad. I don't know which is worse."

"Not necessarily," Arthur said. "Anything linking you to the fire is going to be incinerated before long."

"Yeah. Including you and Sargon."

"Shame, eh? Especially when we got no intention of telling." He winked at Sargon. "Isn't that right buddy?"

The boy was hunched over, staring disconsolately at the floor.

"Sargon?"

"What you did was foolish," the boy said eventually. "But it was a genuine mistake."

His voice lowered to a whisper.

"Unlike you, *my* actions can never be forgiven."

"What are you talking about?"

"I, too, have a story to tell. It may also be my last chance to confess."

He took a deep breath.

"For a start, I am *not* Sargon Danaan."

28

"I was taken from home when I was very young," he continued. "My abductors trained me to be a soldier, though I was a mere child. Under their instruction, I became a hardened warrior. I even killed for them."

All trace of Sargon's thick accent had gone and his phraseology had changed too.

"You don't have to tell us this," Arthur began. But Courage laid a hand on his arm.

"I think he does."

"One day, we abducted a small refugee convoy from the north on its way through our territory. In it was a boy about my age. Sargon Danaan. He would have been just another anonymous captive and not even caught my eye if it were not for one thing."

"What was that?"

"We looked so much alike we might have passed for brothers."

The boy bit his lip.

"Yet we couldn't have been more different. Sargon was selfless and heroic. He kept the rest of his group's spirits up by clowning and making jokes. Shared his meagre rations with them and argued with the guards to get more, even though he risked a rifle butt to his head."

Courage and Arthur stayed mute, letting their friend unburden himself.

"I was given the task of searching the refugees and found identification papers hidden in Sargon's shoe. I laughed and said he'd never get the chance to use them. But Sargon Danaan already knew that."

The boy's eyes were dark shadows.

"He urged me to hide the papers and use them myself one day. Said I did not have to live this life but could escape and take on his identity. All this for someone who had subjected him to abuse and pain."

He began to cry.

"For the first time, I saw goodness in a place where it had been forgotten. I knew this boy could not be my enemy."

"You didn't kill him, did you?" Courage asked, appalled. "You couldn't have."

"No. There was an air strike on our base that night," the teen replied. "Our building was hit and went up in flames. I tried to get Sargon out but his legs had been badly burned and he refused to leave his comrades. I was hurt too and didn't want to die, so I left him struggling to save the others and ran."

He wiped away tears.

"I escaped in the confusion, walked through the night to a hospital camp and handed over his papers. Though we were nearly identical in looks, my accent would give me away, so I refused to speak until I had learned English. But, every day, more refugees arrived. It was only a matter of time before someone who knew the real Sargon Danaan would expose me as an imposter."

His voice dropped to a whisper.

"My commanders had to believe I died in the strike. If they knew I had deserted, they would kill what remained of my family. So I fled again and have been running ever since."

"That's why you won't leave me behind," Arthur said. "Now I get it."

"I won't abandon another person to protect my own skin."

"That's not what he means," Courage knelt by the boy. "You aren't pretending to be Sargon Danaan anymore. You've *become* him."

"I'm not worthy of the name. As you guessed, Arthur, my English is nearly perfect. I had intended to ditch this persona once I left the hospital and assume a new identity."

He refused to look up.

"I want to be anyone except me."

"I know how *that* feels," Arthur grunted.

"Don't be so insensitive, you jerk." Courage punched him again. "Show your friend some respect."

"You're willing to forgive me?" Sargon asked warily.

"I'm the person who set the bloody building on fire. What do *you* think?"

"Arthur?"

"Well, you're both making me feel better about myself, if that helps." Arthur tapped his lip thoughtfully. "So… shall we sing a quick burst of Kumbaya or get on with staying alive?"

"Then stop acting all superior and get that brain whirring," Courage grunted. "You took on the job, after all."

"OK. I've been thinking while you two were feeling sorry for yourselves. We're going to use the service elevator."

Sargon stayed silent.

"No sarcastic comment?" Arthur prompted. "That's not like you."

"It's a stupid idea," Sargon replied in a monotone voice. "The elevator will be switched off by now."

Arthur leaned over and whispered in his ear.

"C'mon buddy. I'm the bitter, sarcastic one. But, like it or not, you're the guy who never stops joking in the face of danger. The person who keeps our spirits up. We *need* Sargon Danaan."

"I'm tired of pretending," the boy said forlornly. "Anyway, making light of the situation won't change it. We cannot use the lift."

"Actually, I meant to climb down the shaft."

Sargon glanced at Courage. She smiled encouragingly at him and clasped her hands together. He noticed the lines of tension around her fearful eyes.

As his companions watched, the boy visibly began to pull himself together. He smoothed his hair back, slowly straightened and took several deep breaths. Then his morose expression vanished and the transformation was complete.

"What a most splendid notion!" He grinned from ear to ear, his broad accent suddenly returning. "You are like a hospital Houdini."

"Welcome back, my friend." Arthur's relief was palpable

"Let us get our figure skates on, then." Sargon grabbed his axe and strode to the lift. Freed from the cast, he was more mobile than before, though his face betrayed the pain his foot was causing. Or perhaps it was the recollections he had brought into the open.

He pushed his blade into the crack between the doors.

"I am experiencing a feeling of Degas Vu." he snorted.

But, unlike the door on the roof, these were easily prised apart. A cloud of smoke billowed out and Sargon leaned over the edge.

"It is hot, yet there is no blaze!" he crowed. "The shaft is sealed and, anyway, there is nothing in it to burn. It is a bit fuggy but I can make out a lift at the bottom."

"What happens when we reach it?"

"Most elevator cars have a trapdoor on the top. If we climb through it, we can exit and be in the basement below the fire."

"Will we be able to breathe, though?" Courage helped Arthur over to the lift. "It looks pretty inhospitable down there."

"That is because we are *in* a hospital," Sargon cackled. "Get it?"

"No need to go into comic overdrive," the girl sighed. "One more gag like that and you'll be testing the drop with my foot on your backside."

"It will be difficult. But possible if we proceed swiftly enough." Sargon looked approvingly at their knee pads and gloves. "We shall grip the cables with our legs and this protection will prevent the cables flaying off our skin. Probably."

"Not me, obviously," Arthur said. "I'll have to go hand over hand."

"You will not manage eight stories in that fashion." Sargon shook his head. "Even if you could, our progress would be too slow. Fumes would overcome your lungs long before we reached our destination."

"He'll go on my back," Courage said.

"That will not work either." Sargon stared into the abyss. "I fear neither of us are strapping enough to carry Arthur that distance."

"Don't dilly dally then." The boy waved them away. "Climb down and send help."

"You must proceed alone," Sargon told Courage. "I cannot leave my annoying chum."

"No. You go." Courage stepped back. "I'll stay with him."

"What is with you two?" Arthur exploded. "You join Martyr's Anonymous or something? You have a chance to make up for your mistakes. I don't!"

Neither of his companions moved.

"Get out of here!" the boy snapped. "Stop treating me like a bloody invalid!"

Courage and Sargon raised their eyebrows.

"All right, that was a daft thing to say. But see sense, will you?"

"We're going together, Arthur," Courage said evenly. "Or not at all. So, come up with something else."

Arthur closed his eyes and thought hard.

"All right. We're going to take off our belts."

"I agree the situation is sorely needing some levity." Sargon unclipped his buckle. "Will having my pants around my ankles improve our chances?"

"It'll certainly cheer *me* up," Courage chuckled.

"And there's no chance of my jeans falling down." Arthur unfastened his own belt. "Since I've been spending most of the night in a horizontal position."

"Already guessed what you're up to." Courage took the belts and fastened them together. "You and Sargon are going down face to face, with these looped round your waists to keep your bodies together. Yeah?"

"Actually, I was kind of hoping I'd be tied to you," Arthur smirked.

"I have no objection to that." The girl laughed out loud this time. "I think Sargon's in more in need of a hug, though."

"I am far too macho for that," the boy retorted. "I will do the dirty deed but Arthur must keep his ugly mug a respectable distance from my own."

29

Brandon and Tyres sat in the basement, grumpy and exhausted. Their faces were caked with soot and they smelled of charred wood and stale sweat.

"We look like a couple of pandas." Brandon tried to make light of the situation. "Ever seen the ones at the zoo, on loan from China? I've gone once or twice but the queue is always too long. Anyway, you have to pay extra. I prefer the wombats."

"We should be up there helping." Tyres refused to be drawn out of her sulk. "The pandas are more endangered than we are down here."

"I thought we did pretty well. Don't we deserve a rest?"

"*You* did well, considering it's your first proper outing. But I'm a woman. I have to go twice as hard to prove myself."

"I'm sure that's not true." Brandon put down the walkie-talkie and searched his pockets. "Everyone knows you're the best driver at the station. That's how you got your nickname, isn't it?"

"I got the moniker because I was a few pounds overweight when I joined the service," Tyres scoffed. "You've a lot to learn."

"Oh." Brandon was still patting his uniform. "You look pretty fit now."

"Lugging a hose up and down stairs every week will do that." Tyres pretended she hadn't noticed his clumsy flattery. "What the hell are you looking for?"

"Pound coins. I saw a vending machine down here and I'm starving." He gave up searching. "You got any change?"

"Just force the bloody thing open. Come to think of it, I wouldn't mind some chocolate."

"I can't." Brandon looked shocked. "That's stealing. From a hospital!"

"Considering the millions of pounds of damage already done to this place, I hardly think it'll make any odds." She stomped off, hiding a smile. "Don't worry, you big Boy Scout. I'll do it myself."

"You think they have Kit-Kats?" Brandon relented. "I love Kit-Kats. Toblerones are good too, though they're a bit hard on the gums."

He followed her down the corridor, completely forgetting he had left the walkie-talkie behind.

Outside, the electrical storm had fully hit and forks of lightning were flashing across the sky every few minutes. Yet there was still no rain. Just dry howling gusts.

Markham Silver and Bailly Cousin were staring at the Eyesore's fourteenth floor in consternation.

"That big hole is causing a real convection funnel," Markham said. "I don't like it."

Bailly knew exactly what he meant. Eden Heights was wrapped in an arctic embrace, drawing heat upwards through the whole building and out of the gap. And, it was taking the fire with it, igniting more floors. The few remaining ladders were still pouring water on the conflagration, but it had risen above the limits they could reach – both inside and outside. Now flames were wrapping themselves around the structure like a tightening fist.

They were losing the fight.

Another flash lit the night sky, much nearer than any other. It crackled behind the Eyesore, turning it into a looming black silhouette. Bailly ducked instinctively.

"Damn!" he said. "That was pretty close."

"All the lightning rods on the structure will have been destroyed and this damned building is the tallest thing for miles. With bits of metal girder sticking out everywhere." Markham stroked his long chin. "It's going to get struck soon. God knows what havoc that will wreak."

He made a decision.

"Pull your squads out. Right now. We can't save this place."

Bailly got on the radio.

"Red and Blue teams," he said. "The situation is rapidly worsening. Abandon the anchor point and evacuate immediately. Leave the hoses and get out. Over."

"We're on our way." The voice on the other end sounded neither pleased nor resentful. An order was an order. "Over and out."

Bailly signalled for his men outside to shut off the water and climb down from the functioning ladders. He changed frequency and pressed the call button again.

"Tyres? We're abandoning the building. Over."

There was no answer.

"Sally and Brandon. Are you there? Over."

Still nothing.

"Maybe the transmission isn't reaching the basement," Markham suggested.

"I was in touch with them fine last time they were down there." Bailly frowned. "They must have put down the radio."

"That's rather disappointing. Both seemed very capable."

"Everyone makes mistakes, Sir," Bailly said protectively.

"They do," the Deputy Chief grunted. "But in this job, mistakes get you killed."

"I'll fetch them."

As Bailly trudged towards the entrance, he was met by Red and Blue teams emerging from the building, respirators still strapped to their faces. As soon as they were outside, the men tore them off and sucked in lungfuls of fresh night air. Some sank to their knees, overcome by fatigue.

Rather than proceed immediately, Bailly stopped to do a head count and make sure everyone was all right.

It saved his life.

A huge branch of lightning shot out of the sky and hit the Eyesore half way up. Sparks exploded from the building and another column of flame billowed into the air, accompanied by a tortured rumble.

"Run!" Bailly screamed, pulling the nearest man to his feet.

The front of the building seemed to melt, sagging and bending as the concrete began to crumble. A cascade of bricks tumbled earthwards. The fire-fighters pulled together their last dregs of strength, sprinting towards safety.

Trucks reversed in a mad waltz, gobs of earth spouting from spinning wheels, empty ladders swaying.

With a sound like nails on a blackboard, a thirty foot slab dislodged and crashed to the ground, blocking both the hospital entrance and the vehicle ramp.

Bailly stopped and stared at it in dismay. Then he was running again.

"With me!" he yelled to the nearest firemen. He rounded the building, sliding in the mud until he reached the side entrance.

He could see through the broken glass doors that the collapsing floors had brought the fire down with them.

The ground floor was an inferno and there was no way
to get past.

"Grab the hoses and turn on the water again," he
shouted in desperation

"Tyres and Puppy are under that."

30

Sargon leaned into the shaft, grabbed the thickest cable and swung onto it, wrapping his legs around the metal wires. Courage tossed him the double belt.

"Now comes the hard part. Thank God you're light."

She picked Arthur up, both hands under his armpits. Planting her feet wide on the edge of the shaft, she held the boy out, groaning with effort. Arthur grabbed the cable above Sargon's head. The boy pulled him close and clinched the belt around their waists.

"Ready?"

"Absolutely not."

"Me neither," Courage added. "But I suppose we're doing this."

"To the Batmobile!" Sargon deadpanned. "I have always wanted to say that."

He and Arthur began to slide down the shaft.

Courage paused on the edge, trying not to think about the drop. Then she took hold of the cable and followed.

Within seconds, the smoke was stinging their eyes and scratching their lungs. But the floors sped past.

"I'm losing plenty of weight now," Courage groaned. "Think I left my knees on the last floor."

"Will you stop denigrating yourself?" Sargon glanced up at her shapely figure. "You have legs to die for and I should know. I have an exceedingly good view of them."

"Stop making me blush."

The heat in the shaft was becoming oppressive and the trio were finding it hard to inhale without choking. Tiny loose filaments on the cable were shredding their gloves and knee pads. Sargon cried out as one pierced his hand.

There was a loud boom and the whole building vibrated. Courage wrapped her body around the cables as they jerked and shook, while Sargon grabbed Arthur and held on tight.

Brandon and Tyres were sitting by the broken vending machine, hungrily munching their snacks, when the explosion rocked the Eyesore. The roof above them buckled and steam burst from several overhead pipes.

"What the hell was that?"

"Our cue to exit." Tyres dropped the Mars Bar she had been wolfing down and pulled her companion to his feet. "Let's get out of here."

They bolted along the corridors towards the stairs, racing through an environment that had suddenly turned deadly.

Through open doors, they saw the garbage and laundry bins were aflame, molten liquid pouring into them from the twisted chutes. They slammed the doors closed and kept going. Sparks leapt from the mesh of wires on the ceiling, bouncing off their helmets. Brandon scrabbled at his waist for the radio before realising he no longer had it.

And, suddenly, they could go no further.

The passageway ended in a wall of concrete blocks and rubble. One glance told the pair they couldn't make a dent in it.

"Damn. There's no other way out." Tyres sounded strangely dispassionate. "Sorry Puppy. It looks like we're trapped."

"The hell we are." Brandon retorted. "Do you have a master key for the service elevator? Bailly told me that every lift has an emergency override."

"I do." Tyres sounded uncertain. "But we don't know what's waiting for us if we take it."

"Only one way to find out." Brandon calmly turned her around. Paint on the corridor was already starting to blister as heat built up behind the walls. "And there's no doubt what's going to happen if we stay down here. I say we take the chance."

"Lead on Macduff," Tyres said admiringly. "You'll make a fine fire-fighter someday. If this one doesn't kill you first."

The conflagration was already eating through the closed doors, blackening the wood and releasing poisonous fumes. They unclipped respirators from their belts and put them on, then retreated the way they had come.

The end of the corridor was still untouched. Tyres used her key to switch on the elevator and the door slid open. Brandon began loading the spare fire extinguishers inside.

"Keep going." Tyres grabbed an extinguisher. "I'll buy you more time."

She walked briskly back down the passageway to tackle the approaching fire, while Brandon kicked open the largest supply room and scanned the contents.

His eyes lit up.

"Will you look at that?"

In one corner were Mylar rescue blankets, thick silver sheets used to wrap burn victims, with loops to allow rescuers to drag any patient safely over burning ground. There wasn't much call for such specialised equipment, which was probably why they were in the basement.

Well... he certainly needed them now, for they were both flame retardant and heat resistant.

Brandon piled them onto a nearby wheelchair and added a few tubs of thick viscose ointment for treating lesions. That ought to protect their exposed skin.

He pushed the wheelchair into the corridor and upended the contents into the elevator. Tyres was now battling an advancing wall of crackling orange sprites, her body wreathed in a cloud of icy vapour from the extinguisher in her hand.

Brandon reckoned he still had a few more minutes. He tossed his axe into the elevator for good measure and was about to head back to the supply room.

Then he heard voices above.

It couldn't be. Yet, there was absolutely no mistaking the sound.

There were people in the elevator shaft!

"Don't know how much longer I can hold on," Courage cried. The wire had shredded through her gloves and began to cut into flesh. "My hands are bleeding and both arms are coming out of their sockets."

Searing heat was now emanating from the walls, turning the duct into an oven.

"You have to keep going," Arthur shouted. "Or you'll fry."

"You must persevere, Courage." Sargon glanced up. "If you let go now, you will hit us."

"Yeah, but I'll have a soft landing."

"That is the spirit."

"Don't worry. I'm not going to fall and give you the satisfaction of being right."

She began to descend again, giving little yelps of pain.

Three. Two. One. Ground. Basement.

Sargon and Arthur collapsed onto the roof of the lift, nursing friction burns where their protective clothing had been worn away. Seconds later, Courage landed beside them, face white and waxy.

The service hatch flew open and a young man's head appeared, yellow helmet perched on top. Courage gave a squeal.

"Holy shit!" Brandon breathed. "I *knew* you two were in here somewhere! Where on earth did you come from?"

"Made our way down from the roof," Arthur panted. "Decided to take the scenic route."

"We checked up there with a helicopter. There was no sign of you."

"We did not think it wise to hang around," Sargon explained.

"And you picked up a nurse on the way." He gave Courage a winning smile then did a double take. "Hold on a minute, you're just a girl..."

"I get that a lot," Courage sighed. "Right now, I'll be anything you want."

"I am Sargon Danaan." The boy unfastened his belt and gently eased his friend away. "The brazen hussy is Courage and my legless companion is Arthur."

"Brandon Gollege, at your service. I'll get the guy with the normal name first."

The fire-fighter pulled himself into the shaft and hoisted Arthur over one wiry shoulder. "This is what's called a fireman's lift. Self-explanatory, really."

"I'm getting carried by a professional at last," Arthur relaxed. "How on earth did I manage before?"

Brandon wriggled back down, careful not to bang the teen's head against the hatch.

"You even brought a ride for me," Arthur said happily, spotting the wheelchair. "You're very good at what you do."

"You won't say that when you see our predicament." Brandon lowered him into the chair then assisted the others through the hatch. "We're trapped down here. Me and my partner, Sally. Only I call her Tyres. It's a long story."

"You intending to take a trip in this lift?" Courage looked around at the equipment. "Cause it isn't looking great above us."

"Sorry. But there isn't any other…"

He was interrupted by a crash and a chilling scream from around the corner.

31

Brandon grabbed an extinguisher and dashed into the corridor. Courage and Sargon followed him, with Arthur slowly bringing up the rear.

Tyres was crawling towards them, legs and torso on fire. A section of ceiling had collapsed right above her, bombarding the woman with burning plaster. Her respirator had been knocked off and her face was a mask of anguish.

"Get a fire blanket and ointment!" Brandon played a jet of foam over his companion. "They're in the lift."

Courage rushed off and came back with both. Parts of Tyre's uniform had been scorched away, exposing raw, oozing flesh. Brandon lathered on ointment and the woman screamed.

"I got you, Tyres," he murmured soothingly. "I'm here."

"Hold on tight." Courage clasped her hand. "You're going to be all right."

"Are you sure?" Tyres sounded close to panic. "It hurts so bad!"

"I'm sure. Trust me. I'm a... nurse."

Sargon spread out the fire blanket. Courage and Brandon lifted Tyres onto it. As gently as they could, they wrapped the fabric around her body. The woman screamed again, then lapsed into merciful unconsciousness, allowing them to move her further from the fire.

Arthur tried to get closer but there was too much debris in the way. There was nothing he could do but watch.

"Help me get her in the lift," Brandon commanded. "It's a slim chance but we can't reach the stairs and there's no other way out."

"There is." Courage fished a small key from her pocket. She pushed past Arthur to the locked door at the end of the passage, inserted the key and opened it.

"This is the old janitor's room."

"I appreciate you're trying to help," Brandon seethed. "But hiding in there won't buy us more than a few minutes. I'm the expert. You have to do as I say."

"There's a small maintenance bay underneath, with a hatch leading to a sewage tunnel." Courage came loping back. "Goes all the way to the main hospital where there's a ladder up to their basement."

"How do you know that?"

"Used to live here."

"I stand corrected," Brandon apologised. He leaned over the comatose woman. "Hear that Sally? We have a way out, after all. You'll make it, I promise."

"We must hurry." Sargon peeled back the blanket and inspected Tyre's wounds. "The lady is in a sorry state and must have medical attention immediately."

"You said it was a sewage tunnel?" Brandon said. "How deep?"

"Waist high, I think. I've never been down there. Only looked."

"If we can't keep Tyres above the water, she'll get badly infected," the fireman groaned. "She's covered in open sores."

He looked around, close to panic.

"Arthur's wheelchair won't get down there either."

"Then you carry him." Courage stuck out her chin. "Sargon and I will find a stretcher and hold your friend over the muck."

"That won't work." Brandon shook his head. "You two are so exhausted, you can barely stand."

"Do not be underestimating us," Sargon retorted. "And we are not leaving Arthur behind."

"I'll come back for him or die trying!" Brandon pleaded. "But we can't all make it in one go. It's not psychically possible."

"I do not doubt your resolve." Sargon stood his ground. "However, the fire will beat you to Arthur and this I cannot allow. I shall carry him myself."

He limped towards the boy.

"One last effort, my friend. We are almost home."

"We got stuck here by mistake." Arthur began to wheel away from him. "That woman came in voluntarily, knowing the risks. You have to save her."

"We will," Courage joined in. "All of us. Together."

"I said I didn't want to be treated like an invalid." Arthur manoeuvred himself into the lift. "What I meant was, I don't want special treatment *because* I'm an invalid. I can't come with you and if you don't accept it, Tyres is dead."

"No. I'm wrong." Brandon held up his hands. "I can carry you and hold the stretcher. You're light and I'm strong."

"I'm taking the lift to the ground floor and see if it's passable. If it is, your friend can be out in minutes."

"And if it's not, you'll be incinerated! I can't put a civilian in that sort of danger, especially not a kid."

"You're not thinking straight!" Arthur's finger was on the button. "If you're killed or injured, *we* won't be able to carry Tyres through the pipe. This is the most sensible option. The *only* option."

Sargon shuffled his feet by the elevator door, a range of emotions playing across his face.

"Here's my chance to finally shine, guys," Arthur said calmly. "Prove I'm not a burden."

"Not your call, I'm afraid." Brandon moved forward to grab him. "I'm going and that's that."

"Arthur makes the plans, however awful they may be." Sargon blocked the man's path. "I do what he says."

Though shorter than Brandon, he was burlier and just as determined.

"Sargon!" Courage looked horrified. "You can't let him."

"I'm the boss, remember?" Arthur reminded her. "We agreed."

Behind them, Tyres moved slightly and let out an agonised moan. Brandon clenched his fists.

"Wear my respirator." He wrapped a fire blanket around Arthur and fastened the mask to his face, while Sargon balanced an extinguisher on the boy's knees.

"If there's no way out," Brandon commanded. "Hit lower basement and come straight down. Or I'll kill you myself."

"You get back safe, hear me?" Courage threw her arms around the boy. "I'd kiss you if you weren't wearing that damned contraption."

Arthur slid the mask up.

"Go on then. It's not glued to my face."

The girl pressed her lips against his.

"Jealous?" Arthur winked at Sargon.

"Insanely. You are even better with the damsels than I."

Arthur beamed and pushed the respirator down again.

"God forgive me for doing this." Brandon stuck his helmet on the teen's head and fastened the strap. "My heart says no but my head knows you're right."

He pulled off his gloves and handed them over.

"Put these on. And keep your face turned away from the door when it opens."

"If it's good news, I'll be back in a couple of minutes," Arthur's voice was muffled. "If not, go without me. I can be a bit tardy sometimes."

"All right, but...."

"Stop fussing, will you?" He jabbed the button and the lift door closed.

"I'll find a stretcher and painkillers for Tyres. Bandages as well." Brandon did an about-face and ran off before they could see the tears in his eyes.

"For once, I have no words." Sargon put his arm around Courage's shoulder.

They stood and stared at the door, listening to the elevator ascend.

Arthur got ready with the extinguisher as the cab reached basement one. The doors opened with a ding and he was hit by a wave of heat. But no flames.

"So far, so good." He wheeled forward and peeked out.

Several cars were wrapped in fire and greasy black smoke billowed from their shattered windows. Broken concrete pillars leaned at crazy angles. Electric cables hung from the roof, writhing like plastic snakes with fizzing metal fangs. The stairs and vehicle ramp were blocked, huge sections of the floor had collapsed and a pool of blazing petrol was spreading in all directions.

"Crap. No getting out this way." The teen retreated and punched the button for the ground floor.

The elevator moved up and opened again. A cloud of smoke billowed in but still no fire. Arthur cautiously looked out again.

At the end of the corridor, the reception area was burning fiercely. As he watched, a chandelier plunged from the ceiling and exploded into a thousand shards of glittering glass. There was no way around the inferno.

Arthur let the doors close for a second time and leaned back against his headrest.

He had done his part. He could join the others with a clear conscience.

But, because they were his friends, they'd insist on carrying him to safety. He'd slow them immensely and one slip would dump Tyres in raw sewage. All right, he didn't know her and it was her job, saving people. She'd known the risks.

So what? Sargon was a killer and Courage a thief. Yet they had risked their lives a dozen times for someone *they* just met. They all deserved a chance. And that slim opportunity would evaporate if he returned.

"Time to man up." Arthur hefted Brandon's axe and used the handle to press the button for the only level where he was certain there would be no fire.

The top floor.

-Part 4-

> *Sometimes your only available transportation is a leap of faith.*
>
> Margaret Shepard

32

Sargon and Courage listened as the elevator continued ascending.

"What's he playing at?" The girl pressed her ear against the door. "He's still going up!"

She began to jab the call button.

"Any sign of your pal?" Brandon appeared behind them, face etched with worry.

"Arthur is not coming back," Sargon said. "I imagine he is heading for the roof again."

"*Why?*"

"It is the one place he can be sure is not ablaze, after all the water we dumped on it. And you mentioned a rescue helicopter. He will hope for that to arrive in time."

"The little fool won't make it," Brandon stammered. "Floors six and seven are completely engulfed."

"Don't you dare!" Courage whirled round and thumped his chest. "You've no idea what he's capable of."

"And the helicopter won't think to look on the roof again. Not unless we make it out alive to tell the pilot."

211

"Then we had better do so," Sargon said deter-minedly.

"You bet your ass we will. I'll get the chopper up there if I have to fly the damned thing myself."

Brandon didn't mention that there was virtually no way to affect a rescue in this storm. No need to dash their hopes further.

Another chunk of masonry crashed into the corridor and the blaze leapt forwards several feet, a pouncing red predator. The trio grabbed the loops on the fire blanket and dragged Tyres into the janitor's room.

"Smear ointment on any cuts you have." Brandon grabbed a jar from the nearest shelf and handed it to Courage. "They're not too deep, so you'll be protected from the sewage."

He pointed to Sargon's bandaged foot.

"You can wear Tyre's boots." His lip quivered. "We used to tease her about having big feet."

They gently removed the footwear and Sargon put them on.

Brandon opened the trapdoor and a putrid smell rose up, making them gag. A dirty brown stream flowed sluggishly through the darkness below them.

"Your mate saved my partner's life," he said grimly. "Let's do our best to save his."

Inside the elevator, Arthur pulled the remaining sil-ver sheets over his body. Then he set off several fire extinguishers as the lift creaked slowly upwards. Foam began to rapidly rise, covering his feet and then his knees. He glanced up at the buttons, memorising their exact locations.

The elevator reached floor six. The door pinged, open and a broiling wave of fire surged into the metal box. The foam fizzled and curdled, searing heat evaporating the ointment on the teen's forehead and cheeks, blistering them instantly. Keeping his face turned away, as instructed, he pushed the axe handle through the inferno and pressed the top floor again.

The door slowly closed, cutting off the deadly crackling tendrils.

Arthur peeled off the top blanket, all but destroyed by this blaze and set off the remaining extinguishers. He turned the last one on himself, spraying his face and torso.

The door opened on the next level.

He gripped the tank, still pouring a foaming torrent over him, and clutched it to his chest. Another wave of fire cascaded into the lift, completely enveloping the boy. The oxygen mask began to melt. Arthur pulled it off, holding his breath to stop his lungs being boiled. His lips blistered and burst as, eyes closed, he thrust out his arm once more and hit the button.

The door slowly shut, shielding him from the hell outside. He gulped hot air, tore the smoking helmet from his head and beat out flames licking up the elevator walls.

If the next floor was this bad, he wouldn't survive.

But the lift continued upwards. The parts of the building that had collapsed were at the front and the service elevator was at the rear. It ground against the shaft, shuddering and screeching, but didn't stop. Finally, he reached his destination.

"Top floor," Arthur rasped. The elevator opened onto the blackened passageway. "Ladies lingerie, complaints department and general mayhem. We're having a fire sale."

He rolled out and began to traverse the corridor, littered with broken furniture and detritus. The wheels on his chair wobbled alarmingly, rubber treads melting away despite the extinguisher foam. His skin felt cooked and every part of his body throbbed but he carried on.

Ten yards from the stairs leading to the roof, the wheelchair collapsed and he spilled onto the floor.

"You did well." He patted the conveyance affectionately as if it were a dying horse. "But I'll write to the manufacturer and suggest the next model be made of asbestos."

He fixed his eyes on the stairs and began to crawl.

Courage, Sargon and Brandon managed to lower Tyres into the sewage tunnel. The roof was low and Brandon especially had to hunch over. Fortunately, Courage had been wrong and the foetid water was only knee deep. They splashed slowly along in the darkness, holding the loops of the fire blanket, keeping the woman just above the stream. The smell was even more overpowering in the confined space and they fought not to retch.

"Are you two all right?" Brandon asked. His own back was aching from the unusual position. "You must be on your last legs."

"I admit this has been a trying day." Sargon was hirpling badly and Courage coughed violently every few seconds. It was obvious both teens were running on empty.

"Only a few yards more," Brandon cajoled, trying to keep their spirits up. "You're both going to be famous after this. Get in the newspapers and everything. Won't that be cool?"

Sargon and Courage looked at each other.

"When we reach safety," the boy said. "I would appreciate if you did not mention our part in this and let us vanish."

"What?" Brandon spluttered.

"We were never here," Courage added. "Tyres is so out of it, she won't remember we ever met."

"Are you for real?" Brandon shifted his weight and sought better purchase on the makeshift stretcher. "You'll both be heroes."

"Like superheroes, we wish to keep our identities a secret," Sargon insisted. "You must concentrate on saving Arthur and forget about us."

"Why all the cloak and dagger stuff?" Brandon stopped. He suddenly remembered that Courage had a key for the janitor's room, right next to the burnt-out fuse boxes.

"Wait. You didn't… cause all this, did you?"

Courage stayed quiet but a guilty look flitted over her face.

"Well done, Sherlock Holmes." Sargon jumped to the girl's defence. "I am an incompetent jihadist who could not be bothered walking a hundred yards to kill infidels in the proper hospital. So I blew myself up in an empty one. Then survived."

"Sorry. That was an idiotic thing for me to say," Brandon reddened. "Especially after all you've been through. I'm a bit frazzled, that's all. It's my first fire."

"Mine too," Courage replied sarcastically. "The truth is, Sargon's an illegal immigrant and I'm a runaway. So will you just promise? I don't have the strength to argue and you owe us."

Brandon hesitated. Letting them walk away unreported went against everything in his training. But they had rescued Tyres and saved him as well.

"I'll do my best."

"That is good enough for me," Sargon nodded. "You seem like an honest fellow."

The group stumbled along in silence until they finally reached a ladder. Sargon climbed to the top and prised off the hatch. Then they manoeuvred Tyres up, Brandon pushing from the bottom, Sargon pulling and Courage, half way up, guiding them.

Eventually, the injured woman lay on the floor of New Collingwood's basement, her breathing ragged and shallow.

"Let us never do this again." Sargon patted Brandon's shoulder. "I'm sorry we cannot send Tyres a get well card."

"Where are you going to go?"

"We'll hang around until we know Arthur is safe," Courage said. "Just don't give us away."

"You have my word." Brandon looked at Courage's sooty visage. "Rub some more dirt on your face to hide your age. With that outfit on, everyone will assume you're the real thing. Sargon will have to disguise himself or find somewhere to hide."

Brandon waited until the pair had staggered off, supporting each other as they went. Then he began to shout.

"Help me! I have a badly hurt fire-fighter here!"

Within minutes, hospital staff arrived. As they carried Tyres to the burn ward, Brandon cricked his neck and headed back towards the Eyesore.

33

Arthur reached the top of the stairs and heaved himself onto the roof, arms aching. There was a howling maelstrom over him and a fork of lightning briefly illuminated banks of storm clouds, almost hidden behind a black curtain.

After all that exertion, he was back where he started and in a far worse condition.

He leaned back against the concrete block. Brandon had mentioned a helicopter but he couldn't depend on that. Not in this weather.

He needed an alternative strategy.

Arthur lurched forwards and began to crawl again.

Markham Silver and Bailly Cousins were gloomily watching their men's efforts to douse the ground floor when they felt a tap on their shoulders.

"I miss anything interesting?"

"Puppy!" Bailly threw his arms around the rookie. "How in God's name did you get out?"

He stepped back quickly.

"Why do you smell like a toilet?"

"Where's Sally Hampton?" Markham got right to the point, as always.

"Being treated for burns in the main hospital. She's in bad shape but they say she'll make it." Brandon grabbed a water bottle from a nearby table, took a long swig, and then emptied the rest of the contents over his body. "We found a sewage tunnel and used that."

"Good thinking." Bailly turned to leave. "I'd like to go check on Tyres, if that's all right, Chief?"

"No. There's a boy on the roof." Brandon grabbed his arm. "It's Arthur Lawson."

"But you checked up there!"

"He was in the basement with me but he's a wheel-chair user. He couldn't manage the tunnel and the place was turning into an inferno, so he took the service elevator to the top."

Markham and Bailly looked warily at each other.

"I know what you're thinking," Brandon said. "But if anyone could make it, it's that kid. He got from the damned top all the way to the basement in the first place."

"On his own?" Markham sounded deeply suspicious.

"I'll make a full report later." Brandon crossed his fingers. "Right now, I'd like permission to accompany the chopper and try to rescue him."

Another bolt of lightning rent the atmosphere.

"It's the pilot's call, I'm afraid," Markham said warily. "It may not be possible for him to even get in the air with all this going on."

"May I have a shot at persuading him?"

"You've earned that right." Markham handed him a walkie-talkie. "Just don't lose another radio, there's a good lad."

Brandon flushed bright red and ran off.

"That was a bit harsh, Chief," Bailly said reproach-fully.

"Oh, he's a sound lad," Markham conceded. "But the boy needs to know what he did wrong more than what he did right. Worked for the last rookie I met who had so much potential."

The Deputy Chief nudged his second in command.

"Guy called Bailly Cousins, if I remember rightly."

It was Bailly's turn to blush.

Brandon reached the helicopter. The pilot and winch man were sitting on stools a few feet away, eat-ing sandwiches.

"You again." The pilot looked surprised. "Where's your friend?"

"In intensive care."

"Sorry, mate."

"And there *is* a boy on the roof."

The pilot put down his snack and climbed into the helicopter, followed by the winch man.

"You coming?" he glanced over his shoulder. "The more the merrier, even if you smell like a skunk's bum."

"Chief Markham said you might not want to go." Brandon vaulted into the seat beside them. "That it was too dangerous."

"We don't and it is. Never stopped us before."

The pilot punched a few buttons and the rotors began to slowly turn.

"Seems you have company. Bit of a ladies' man, huh?"

A nurse was sprinting towards them, bent low to avoid the blades. She reached the Dolphin and climbed into the rear.

"No. No. No." Brandon tried to push Courage back out. "You can't come."

"I'm a trained paramedic," The winch man agreed. "You look like you've just been dragged out of a chimney, doll."

He was right. Courage's face was so blackened with grime there was no way they could tell she was only a teenager. Yet, somehow, she seemed to have acquired a clean uniform.

"Arthur is disabled," the girl refused to budge. "He needs specialist treatment and, anyway, I know him."

"Fair enough," the pilot shrugged. "Too late anyway. We're off."

He pulled back on the stick and the chopper rose unsteadily into the air.

The helicopter's second foray was infinitely worse than its first. The wind was much stronger and flung the Dolphin around like a kite. Even strapped in, the occupants banged against each other, the pilot and winch man's helmets repeatedly clonking together like some crazy Newton's Cradle. Courage squeezed her eyes shut and seemed to be praying.

And still they rose. Up through churning veils of smoke, thick as scrunched tissue. They finally reached the rim of Eden Heights and attempted to hover over the building. But each new gust sent the chopper off at a tangent.

"I can barely control the machine," the pilot warned, arched over the controls.

"Do your best." The winch man pointed. "There he is."

Arthur was propped against the davit, waving with both hands.

"You sure you want to risk this?" The pilot shouted, joystick shuddering in his hands. "Your call."

"I'll give it a try." The winch man unfastened his safety belt. "Can't promise anything."

"Where's Sargon?" Brandon mouthed to Courage while the pair were occupied.

"Looking for dry clothes," she shouted in his ear, voice almost drowned out by the ululating rotors. "I stole mine from the staff room in the main hospital."

"You two are incredible. Where are you getting your reserves of stamina from?"

"Same place as you lot." She indicated the firemen below, still battling to save the building.

"Ready to go." The winch man had attached the harness he was wearing to a cable. "Nursie? Stay well back from the door and hold onto the struts."

"Like my life depended on it." The girl gripped two iron bars above her seat. "Which, judging by your friend's driving, is all too possible. I shall be buying him some L plates when we reach dry land."

Brandon smiled despite their predicament. Courage sounded just like Sargon.

The winch operator slid open the side door and a howling whine filled the cockpit. Courage's hair whipped around her face as a gritty wind billowed through the chopper. The man punched a button on his belt and stepped into the void.

Arthur watched with bated breath as a tiny figure began to descend like a spider on a steel thread. The further he got from his helicopter, the more he swung, completely at the mercy of the elements. By the time he had descended thirty feet, he was hurtling around the sky like a trick Yo-Yo. The Dolphin plunged down several yards and then swept up again.

As it attempted to get closer, the dangling rescuer played out more cable. He soared towards the teen, so low Arthur could make out every feature of the man's terrified face.

He shot past, almost colliding with the jagged remains of the water tower, then returned even faster, whirling round and round, arms outstretched in a vain attempt to steady himself.

"Stop it, you idiot!" Arthur waved again. "There's no way you can reach me."

The winch man had already reached the same conclusion.

"I'm coming back up." His voice crackled over the radio. "It's not physically possible to get the kid."

"But you're so close!" Courage sobbed, forgetting she didn't have a headset. "You can't give up!"

"I've seen that guy pluck a sailor from twenty foot waves in a hurricane," the pilot shouted. "If he can't get them, he leaps into the water and holds the guy afloat until a boat arrives. This is a different ball game entirely. He lands on the roof? He'll break every bone in his body."

"Can't he use a parachute?"

"Helicopters don't carry them," The pilot jerked a thumb upwards. "Parachutes and blades don't mix and, anyway, we fly too low for them to open in time."

He pulled sharply back on the joystick and the chopper soared away, the rotors shrieking in protest.

"I'm sorry. You'll have to save this guy another way."

34

The helicopter landed with a thud.

"Thanks for trying, you two," Brandon said gratefully. "You went above and beyond the call of duty."

"As did you. Apologies that we couldn't produce a better result."

Courage followed the fire-fighter as he ducked under the rotors and trudged resignedly towards his superiors' command post.

"Arthur's up there all right," he reported bitterly. "We couldn't reach him, though."

"That's what I figured," Markham said. "So I ordered the hundred foot aerial platform round the back of the building, where the fire is weakest. Only... the operators insist it can't be fully extended in this weather."

"Tell them to try, eh?" Courage said brusquely. "All it can do is break - but Arthur's going to die if you don't give it a go."

Brandon waved at her to be quiet.

"Yes. I noted that you took up a civilian." The Deputy Chief's look turned frosty. "How many safety rules are you intending to ignore today?"

"There will be time for recriminations later," Brandon said defiantly. "The... eh... nurse is right. What's a bit of equipment compared to a human life?"

"Not just one life. A man would have to be on the platform when we send it up. If it breaks apart..."

He left the sentence unfinished.

"I'm willing to risk it, Sir," Brandon said. "I had a chance to save Arthur. I didn't do it because I was concentrating on Tyres."

"It's too dangerous."

"Please," Brandon pressed. "Arthur only took the lift so me and Tyres would have a proper chance. I couldn't live with myself if I didn't give it every effort."

The Deputy Chief pondered this. Came to a decision.

"Tell the operators we're sending a volunteer round," he instructed Bailly. "Brandon's right. We can't abandon the kid."

He grabbed the rookie's gloveless hands.

"Get your nurse to bandage those first. You got a couple of bad burns yourself."

Brandon stared at his palms. He had so much adrenaline pumping around his body he hadn't even noticed the wounds.

"I don't have time!"

"If you can't grip things properly, you'll be useless. Do as I say, boy."

"I'll fix it." Courage pulled Brandon away before he could object again and led him to the nearest engine.

"Show me where you keep the first aid kit."

"You're not a real nurse, remember?"

"Maybe. But I'm getting plenty of practice."

Brandon pushed away two spare uniforms hanging in the cab, fetched a red bag with a cross on the front from a hatch and tipped out the contents. Courage applied salve and carefully wrapped his hands, while the fire-fighter fumed with impatience.

"Can't you go any faster?"

"Yeah, yeah. You're in a hurry to die. But I'm trying to do this properly." The girl's own hands were shaking. "Cut me some slack, will you?"

"I'm sorry. I know how tired you must be."

"Apology accepted." Courage finally finished, then stepped back and admired her handiwork.

"Not a bad job."

Brandon leapt from the cab and raced for the back of the building.

"A thanks would be nice." Courage yelled at his retreating back. "Now, where the hell is Sargon?"

The last time she had seen the boy, he had gone to fetch dry clothes of his own.

She looked at the spare uniforms and her jaw dropped as he remembered what Brandon had told Sargon.

You'll have to disguise yourself.

One coat hanger was empty.

"No! You wouldn't!"

But Sargon was the type of guy who definitely *would*.

Courage climbed down and took off after Brandon.

The rookie rounded the building and stopped in puzzlement. The platform was already extended to almost full height, gyrating alarmingly like a giant pencil balanced on its point. Far above, a fire-fighter was holding onto the railings to stop from being tipped out. Brandon climbed on top of the caboose and yanked the operator's arm.

"It's supposed to be *me* going up."

"Count your blessings that bloke got here first." The man was concentrated on the equipment, sweat streaming down his face. "He'll be lucky to live."

The platform had reached its limit, opposite the 17th floor windows. The hydraulic supports whined as the whole structure swayed. There was a loud crack as the ladder lurched forwards.

"We've got him close a couple of times but the damned glass is reinforced," the operator said. "I'm not sure we can get him down before the machinery seizes and the ladder falls apart."

"Then ram one of the windows!"

"This aerial platform cost £700,000. You don't ram *anything* with it!"

"There's a kid on the roof. You're his last chance."

"Why didn't you say so before?" The operator pushed two handles as hard as he could. The platform shot forwards and crashed into the nearest window, demolishing it. The occupant was catapulted through the gap and vanished from sight.

"Well... he's in."

The man pulled back on the levers and the platform slowly withdrew. But now it hung at an awkward angle, like a hand on a shattered wrist. As they watched in horror, it slowly detached itself from the ladder and plummeted. The fire-fighters crouched behind their equipment as it hit the ground, reduced to a twisted pile of metal. Only the supporting shaft remained, pointing accusingly straight up.

There was a loud bang and steam began to pour from the turntable.

"I'm sorry, but your mate's not coming back the way he went in. This thing's completely screwed."

"Did you recognise him?" But Brandon already knew the answer.

"Don't think it was one of our Glasgow crew, though it was pretty hard to tell. His face was covered in soot and he was wearing a respirator. Said he was called Brandon Gollege, though. Know the name?"

"I do." Brandon climbed slowly down from the caboose. Courage was standing below, looking utterly miserable.

"I think Sargon nicked a fireman's outfit from one of the empty cabs," she said. "It's him up there, isn't it?"

"Of course it is." Brandon's shoulders slumped.

"Now he and Arthur are both doomed."

Brandon returned to Markham and Bailly with a heavy heart.

"What are you doing here?" The men couldn't conceal their surprise. "The platform operator radioed and said one of our men made it into the building. We assumed it was you."

"Someone else beat me to it."

"Is it true they're trapped as well?"

"The platform came off and the turntable seized," Brandon nodded. "The ladder is stuck pointing straight up. It's useless."

Behind them, Bailly was talking urgently on the radio.

"All our men are accounted for, as far as I can tell," he said. "I can't work out who went up. He doesn't seem to have a radio."

Brandon crossed his fingers.

"Eh… I'm pretty sure that 'fireman' is actually the other missing boy, Sargon Danaan. He went to fetch his pal."

"And those Glaswegian idiots let him on the platform!" Bailly choked. "What were they thinking?"

"He was impersonating me. They wouldn't have known he wasn't one of our own. He's a big kid and he had on a stolen uniform and respirator."

"And how do you know all this?" Markham fixed Brandon with a withering stare. "I get the feeling a lot more happened in that basement than you're telling."

"You'll have my full report tomorrow, along with my letter of resignation." Brandon held his stare. "In the meantime, we have two boys to save."

"Godammit!" Bailly thumped the table. "We can't get up and they can't get down. What are we going to do?"

"Get the keys for the platform truck." Markham pushed Brandon away. "Drive it as close to the building as you can manage."

For the first time, he looked truly uncertain.

"Obviously Arthur can't jump but maybe the kids could.... slide out a plank to the ladder or something. Crawl along it."

As he spoke, another blast of wind hit, almost knocking over their makeshift table.

"Not in these conditions, Chief. The currents up there were strong enough to knock a three ton helicopter around like it was made of plywood."

"I'm open to suggestions."

"I'll climb the ladder by hand," Brandon said. "Use a Halligan bar to pull it closer to the window and attach it somehow."

"I'm talking about reasonable suggestions," Markham glowered. "That's suicide and I won't allow it."

"I'll tie a line from my belt to the top of the apparatus. If I fall, the worst that can happen is I'll swing back and hit it. Get a few cuts and bruises."

"Or a broken neck," Bailly muttered. "I strongly oppose this course of action."

"A fifteen year old boy with an injured foot made it in there." Brandon stuck out his chin. "How will it play in the papers when they find out we didn't make as much effort as he did?"

"Touché," Markham replied. "I'll still be expecting your resignation tomorrow. Unless you die, of course."

"Understood." Brandon saluted and turned to go.

"And you can get back to the main hospital." Bailly pointed at Courage. "Civilians are meant to be behind the cordon."

"I'm here now and I'm staying," the girl shot back. "It looks like you might need a nurse."

"I haven't time to argue," the station officer said angrily. "Go with Puppy if you're so determined. You can scoop up his damned remains when he falls."

"Bailly, keep every man you have pouring water on that fire," the Deputy Chief instructed.

"Then pray for a miracle."

35

Sargon made his way along the hazy corridors, shimmering with heat. The water from the fallen tower had long since evaporated and the blaze was gaining momentum again. He passed wards filled with flames, dancing like unholy crimson shadows, shutting each door as he went. He didn't think it would buy him much time.

Sargon tore off his respirator and broke into a sprint, ignoring the pain in his leg. He ran up the last set of stairs and burst onto the roof. Buffeted by the roaring wind, he shouted Arthur's name.

"About time!" The boy was still propped against the broken davit a few yards away. "I was thinking of taking up knitting."

His eyes widened.

"*Sargon*? Is that *you*?"

"You were expecting Mary Poppins?" Sargon stomped over. "I have been saving your crispy butt all day. I could not leave your rescue to a bunch of amateurs, so I came up on an extendable platform."

"Great!" Arthur enthused. "Where is it?"

"It broke."

"*What*?"

"Once again, I fear nobody else is coming." Sargon crouched by his friend. "You saw what happened to the helicopter. Still, I am sure you have worked out a cunning scheme of your own to get us down."

"Of course." Arthur's scalded face was lined with exhaustion. "I'll sit on your back and flap both arms as hard as I can."

"Excuse my bad-tempered expression," Sargon grimaced. "I am laughing inside, of course."

"Is Courage all right?"

"She is safe. Now stop pulling off my legs and tell me the real plan."

"You won't like it."

"I will love it, I assure you. Especially when the alternative is waiting for the Eyesore to collapse. It now contains more holes than Swiss cheese in a string vest."

Arthur pointed to the giant tarpaulin covering half the roof. It rose and fell like some giant lung, straining against its moorings, only the guy ropes preventing the wind from hoisting it into the void.

"We're going to use that as a parachute."

"You have surpassed yourself with this preposterous idea," Sargon grumbled. "I absolutely, totally hate it."

Brandon and Courage met the operators at the platform truck. One of them handed him a coil of rope and the other a Halligan bar - a steel rod with a hook at one end.

"Line's about twenty feet," he said. "Any longer and it'll be too heavy to carry. Still one hell of a climb, even without the extra weight."

"Any advice?" Brandon asked one of the men.

"Yeah. Don't fall."

"It's your show now," the other added. "We've been ordered to take over the extra hoses." He looked puzzled. "I'm not sure why. This is our area of expertise."

Brandon knew exactly why. Markham was vainly trying to hide the identity of the stranded 'fireman' from as many people as possible.

He climbed into the cab, Courage scrambling after him.

"Want me to drive?"

"Do you even have a licence?"

"I've been surviving on the streets, genius. I can hot-wire a bloody car."

"No need. I have a key."

Brandon gunned the engine to life. He drove in a circle and parked the vehicle so close to the building that its flanks almost scraped the brickwork.

"Stay here," he said. "Any more chunks of the Eyesore fall off, you get this piece of junk out of the firing line, so it doesn't end up flattened."

"You got it, handsome. Good luck."

Brandon jumped out of the cab and almost collided with Markham Silver. A few feet behind him, Bailly Cousins was talking urgently into his radio, as always.

"We're your new back up crew." The Deputy Chief smiled thinly. "The less anyone knows about who's really up there, the better. Besides, we never get to see any action these days."

"If Markham was twenty years younger, he'd be going himself," Bailly grumbled. "Me too, only you'd have to tape this damned walkie-talkie to my ear. Never get promoted, Puppy. It's too stressful."

"Thank you, guys! It means a lot to me."

"Please address me as Sir. I won't tell you again." Markham climbed onto the top of the vehicle with Brandon.

"Despite your flagrant disregard for the rules we live by, your vim is rather an inspiration." He fastened one end of the rope to the fire-fighter's belt with a steel clip. "If you can provide me with a plausible explanation for your actions after this is over, you might even keep your job."

"You really think I'll make it?" For a second, Brandon looked exactly as he felt. A frightened young man, taking on a mammoth task that might snuff out his life.

Markham looked ashamed.

"Give me the rope." He held out his hand. "Bailly's right. I'm the one who should go. Not some raw recruit, no matter how brave."

"No offence, Chief." Brandon pulled himself together. "But I'm almost forty years younger and a hell of a lot fitter. The offer is appreciated, though."

"At least let me call for a volunteer with more experience."

"No time." The rookie said. "Besides, it's not experience that'll get me up there. It's the dumbness and sense of indestructibility that comes with youth."

He pointed at the top of the ladder, shuddering with each new gust.

"That's why Sargon made it."

And he began to climb.

"Explain how we are to do this," Sargon said patiently. "As if I were an idiot."

"I found some rope, idiot," Arthur replied. "Cut it into equal lengths. Then I fastened them to this."

There was a length of wood beside him, covered in sturdy knots.

"I was just about to tie the other ends to each corner of the tarpaulin."

"It would have taken a great while in your state of leglessness."

"That's why I'm glad you turned up." He handed one rope end to Sargon. "Off you go."

"So here I am, doing your bidding once more." Sargon inched under the tarp and began to wriggle towards the far end.

"I am crawling anyway," he shouted. "You could have done that."

"I could," Arthur settled back. "But it's nice to have a minion again."

Sargon slithered around under the canvas like a frantic mole, fastening the ropes to each corner.

"This is torture," he yelled. "I shall never be able to straighten my back and will spend my days walking like those old people on your triangular road signs."

But Arthur didn't hear, lost in his own unhappy thoughts.

He knew the scheme wasn't going to work.

Sure, the tarp would lift them off the roof. Might even keep them aloft for a few seconds. But, as soon as they were out of range of the rising convection currents, the storm would seize their makeshift parachute and batter it from all directions. Then it would fold in on itself and drop out of the sky.

But it was all he had come up with, for he had finally run out of ideas. What else could they do? The fire was now raging out of control and would soon overwhelm the roof. Anything was better than burning to death.

Another fork of lightning split the clouds, turning them briefly into a greasy yellow panorama. He glimpsed a few stars in the blackness beyond. He knew their names by heart, for there was nothing else to see at night from his room.

Nature was beautiful, he thought. Even in its fury.

He would miss the stars most of all.

Brandon was three quarters of the way up, but the ladder was vibrating like a drill and increasingly difficult to climb. Perspiration was running down his back in rivulets and his scalded palms began to sting.

A tongue of flame knocked out one of the windows and billowed into the air, narrowly missing him. He gave a yelp and doubled his efforts.

When he finally reached the top, he knew his journey had been in vain. The ladder was now swaying backwards and forwards so violently it took all his strength to hold on. There was no way he could hook a window ledge.

But he had to try.

Clutching the rungs with both legs and one arm, he fastened the other end of the rope round his waist to the ladder, then slowly, painstakingly uncoiled it.

Another blast hit the ladder with the force of a boot kicking a football. Brandon lost his grip and toppled backwards. He tightened his calves as he slammed into the support.

In the cab, Courage saw Markham and Bailly gasp. She leaned out and looked up.

Brandon was hanging upside down, like a trapeze artist, still holding the Halligan. As she watched, he snagged one of the upper struts with the hook and slowly pulled himself upright.

"Give up, Puppy," Bailly murmured. "Just give up, for Christ's sake."

But Brandon climbed back to the top and leaned towards the building, grappling hook in one outstretched arm. There was another boom and the windows two floors below erupted in flame.

"Don't look down to see what that was," Markham implored. "It's a rookie mistake. Please. Don't look down."

Brandon looked down.

36

"All tied." Sargon emerged from the tarpaulin. "Now what?"

"I got another axe here."

"Outstanding!" The teen seized the implement in delight. "I shall name you Slicey McSliceface."

"Do you actually know how sinister that sounds?"

"Never mind that. What shall I do with him?"

"Cut the spare lines holding the tarpaulin to the roof. The wind and heat will pull it into the sky, then it will only be anchored by the four corner ropes tied to this plank."

Arthur hooked the davit cable around the length of wood.

"We play out the winch and hold on. Once we're high enough, we unfasten ourselves and float to the ground."

"Can we not reconsider? I am not particularly keen on this experiment."

Arthur indicated over his shoulder. At the front of the building, fingers of fire were creeping over the rim of the roof like glittering, deadly claws.

"Afraid not. Any last requests?"

Sargon mulled this over.

"To be honest," he said nonchalantly. "I would not mind a hug, after all."

"Excuse me? Thought you were too macho?"

This time, there was no light hearted retort.

"The last time someone held me properly, I was eight years old." Sargon picked at his lip. "It was my mother."

"Don't tell me I look like her. That would just be creepy."

"I do not remember her face."

"Ah." Arthur nodded. "Fair enough, then."

"But we will never speak of it, or my tough cookie image will be half baked."

Sargon sat beside his companion and the boys rested their foreheads together.

"Good luck, buddy," Arthur whispered. "See you on the other side."

"You are an excellent liar, my friend," Sargon replied. "But I am well aware we will not live through this."

He tentatively put his arms around the boy.

"Still, we gave it *such* a fine effort."

"That we did." Arthur patted his back. "We fought fire with fire."

"Now that I am suitably mortified, I shall not mind dying so much." Sargon stood up and stuck out his chest. He began to hobble around the giant tarpaulin, cutting the superfluous moorings with his axe.

The tarpaulin was stout canvas and almost sixty square metres. As each tether was sliced, it billowed further into the air, forming an enormous canopy, straining at the corner ropes. The stout plank creaked alarmingly but didn't break.

"It's working so far," Arthur said hopefully.

Sargon finished and came sprinting back. The pair lay across the plank and Arthur pushed the button on the winch, allowing it to play out.

The makeshift parachute, filled with hot air from the burning building, rose into the sky, carrying the teens with it.

Brandon's head spun. Through the billowing smoke, the fire truck looked like a toy - and his companions were smaller than ants. It suddenly hit him that he was a hundred feet in the air, perched atop a sliver of metal that was rocking back and forth like the mast of a sailing ship caught in a typhoon.

He jerked back with a cry, wrapping both arms around the ladder. His throat tightened and his stomach filled with butterflies as he fought not to vomit.

A strange thought leapt, unbidden, into his head.

If he threw up on the Deputy Chief from this height, he'd *really* be in trouble.

Brandon fought down the nausea. He could overcome this. *Had* to.

He forced his mind back to the training he'd received. In the event of a panic attack on a ladder, never look down. Look up.

He tilted his head back and took in the sky.

"No way." His eyes widened. "No bloody WAY!"

An enormous blue bubble was rising over the top of the Eyesore.

On the ground, Markham and Bailly gawped in astonishment. They could just make out two tiny figures sprawled across a plank, dangling from four ropes under an enormous floating awning.

"Christ," Bailly stammered. "Those kids made a parachute. Or is it a balloon?"

"Either way, it's never going to work. Once they get high enough, the storm will tear it apart."

"Break out a life net." Bailly was on the radio again. "Get it round the back of the building on the double!"

"That won't make the slightest difference," Markham said dejectedly. "It's too big a drop."

"It's all we've got!"

There was a throaty bellow as the truck beside them roared into life. The men whirled around.

In the cab, Courage released the hand brake, mouth set in a grim line.

"Sorry Brandon," she muttered. "But you're holding on like an octopus, anyway."

Six mighty wheels spun and the fire truck lurched forward, gathering speed. The canopy had now begun to drift over the edge of the roof, still ascending.

Courage stuck her head out of the window and followed its trajectory.

The sudden movement almost jolted Brandon from his precarious perch. He clung on even more fiercely as the ladder shook and wobbled.

"What the fuck are you guys up to?" he yelled down. "Don't you think being up here is petrifying enough?"

And, suddenly, he understood.

"Go for it, Courage!" he whooped. "Clever girl!"

"We're actually flying!" Arthur screamed in Sargon's ear. "Can you believe it?"

"I believe I may crap myself at any second." His companion's knuckles were white from gripping the ropes. "I would like to get off the ride now."

Below them, the hospital grounds were laid out like a miniature train set and people were scurrying bugs.

"Didn't really think this thing would stay aloft," Arthur shouted gleefully as they drifted further from the building. "I was *so* wrong!"

A gust of wind hit them from the opposite direction.

The canopy shot sideways, lifted, then fell again. Another burst swept in from behind, flinging the improvised parachute into a spin. Sargon shot backwards, his chin thudding against the plank, fingers scrabbling for purchase, as he tried to stop himself from falling.

"Help me, Arthur!"

"Got you!" His companion reached over and yanked him back by the collar. "Hold on, dammit."

"You are thinking I let go on *purpose*?"

The tarpaulin was wrenched to the side again. There was an ugly tearing sound and a massive rent appeared on its surface. Then, with a whistling wail, it began to fall.

The teenagers' screams were lost in the maelstrom.

Courage pushed the accelerator to the floor. Brandon gave a yelp and pressed his face against wood and metal, using every inch of his body to cling on. As the parachute whirled earthwards, the girl spun the steering wheel to meet it.

The ladder ploughed into the canvas and the billowing sheet wrapped itself round its top, obscuring Brandon.

The ropes acted like a pendulum, swinging both teens into the ladder with a sickening crunch. Arthur flung his arm over Sargon and pulled him close, the other hand snatching frantically at the nearest rung. His hands closed around it as his friend slithered from the plank again. The boy was suspended for several heart-stopping seconds before he found purchase as well.

"My fingers are slipping," Arthur cried.

"Never fear." Sargon finally got a proper hold of the rungs and inched his head between Arthur's legs, broad shoulders taking his friend's weight. "My head is now safely up in your butt."

"I wouldn't have put it like that…. But thank God."

Another hole appeared in the tarp right above them, the tip of the Halligan poking through. The rent widened and one boot emerged, then another. Finally, the rest of Brandon appeared, like a baby bird struggling out of an egg.

"You guys all right?"

"Just peachy," Arthur panted. "Taking a few moments to enjoy the view."

"I am most certainly not enjoying the view." Sargon's stifled voice drifted up. "If Arthur breaks wind, I shall most likely go blind."

"Then let's get to the ground before this thing snaps in two."

With Sargon's assistance, Brandon manoeuvred Arthur onto his back and they began to climb down.

Below them, Courage did a little dance as Markham and Bailly came running over. Bailly swept the laughing girl into his arms and gave her a bear hug.

"Stellar driving," he chuckled. "Tyres would be proud of you."

The Deputy Chief took off his helmet and watched the trio making their way carefully towards the ground.

"I'll be damned, Rookie," he said quietly. "Miracles *do* happen."

37

Markham and Bailly helped Brandon and the boys off the truck and onto solid ground.

"I shall never climb so much as a stepladder again." Sargon sank to his knees and kissed the wet grass. "And will be having nightmares at the sight of a candle."

A dozen fire-fighters had already arrived, one of them pushing a wheelchair. More were running towards them from either side of the building. They clapped Brandon's back and surrounded the teens, chattering excitedly. Arthur had a deep cut on his scalp and his face and arms were scalded. Apart from that, the trio seemed remarkably unharmed.

"Magnificent effort, Puppy," Bailly grinned, glancing slyly at Markham. "Don't see how anyone can sack you now. In fact, I'm recommending you for a medal."

"A motion I will support wholeheartedly," the Deputy Chief agreed.

"I'll settle for a Kit Kat," Brandon said gratefully. "Didn't get to finish the last one I had. It's probably melted by now."

The last of the firemen hurried towards them, eager to congratulate Arthur and whichever of their comrades had rescued him from the roof. Soon the boy was surrounded by mucky, smiling faces.

"I've ordered the hoses turned off for good," Bailly said. "There's nobody left in the Eyesore and it's too far gone to save."

As if it had heard, the building gave a shudder and another level buckled. They watched as an avalanche of bricks cascaded down its concrete façade and thudded harmlessly into the mud fifty yards away.

"Good riddance," one man spat vehemently. "Thing should never been built in the first place."

"I owe you an apology. You were an absolute star." Bailly handed Courage a medical kit. "Eh... Can you see to Arthur's head?"

"Yeah, no problem." Courage took out a length of gauze and dressed the wound. "It's going to need stitches, though."

"You're getting pretty good at this," Arthur sniggered through fractured lips. "Missed your real calling."

"My men will escort you boys to the main hospital for proper treatment," Markham said. "The danger may be over but medical staff are still confined to the other side of the cordon. Except for this determined miss, of course."

He tilted his head at Courage. Her face was so grubby all he could really see were two blue eyes under a mask of grime.

"I never did get your name."

"You can address me as nurse. It's protocol."

"Of course." The Deputy Chief rolled his eyes and approached Sargon, who was almost dead on his feet. "And we'll get you to a well-deserved bed, young man, before you pass out."

"I would greatly appreciate it if you would let me walk away." Sargon removed his coat and helmet. "I do not wish to be the centre of attention. It might look better for you as well."

"Too late, my boy," Markham sighed. "A dozen news cameras and God knows how many mobile phones captured your remarkable escapade."

His embarrassment was all too apparent.

"When the press find out we were fooled into sending a fifteen year old up on that platform, we're going to seem mighty incompetent."

His men looked sheepish, suddenly aware of what had really transpired.

"They were filming from a distance," Sargon said. "It is night and I was dressed as a fireman. If you act quickly to deceive them, your bacon may still be saved."

"I don't understand. You'll be a national hero. On TV and everything."

"Exactly." The boy replied wearily. "Where I shall soon be exposed as an illegal immigrant, using a fake name, and a former child soldier to boot. When my true identity is revealed to the world, I shall be deported and my family back home killed in reprisal for me deserting."

"No way *that's* going to happen," Markham bristled. "Not if I can help it."

The throng of fire-fighters nodded in agreement.

"It is not something you can prevent, I am sorry to say. The flames of hatred are as hard to extinguish as this building."

"You have to let him leave," Arthur urged from his wheelchair. "I'll back up any excuse you want to make."

The Deputy Chief seemed doubtful for a few seconds. But Markham Silver didn't do indecisive, so the moment quickly passed.

"Put the uniform back on, Pronto," he told Sargon. "It's the only way you'll get out of here unnoticed."

He beckoned to Bailly.

"You're about the same size and build as the lad. We'll say you were the one who went up and parachuted back with Arthur."

"I can't take credit for something I didn't do!" Bailly stammered.

"You'll follow my orders." The Deputy Chief commanded. "Not because it makes us look good but to save this youngster from getting shafted."

He pulled himself up to his full height, put his arm around Sargon, and turned to the assembled ranks.

"Speak now if you have a problem with that." His voice was authority personified. "Anyone think this young hero deserves to be treated like a criminal and lose his nearest and dearest? After what he did?"

"No, Sir!" The men cried in unison.

"And you, nurse?"

"My lips are sealed," Courage replied emphatically.

"What will you tell the reporters and police, Arthur?" The Deputy Chief sized him up. "You're just a kid and they can be quite... aggressive."

"Don't even worry about it," the boy said without a trace of hesitation. "I'm an excellent liar and not the type to be intimidated."

He put on a look of wide-eyed, sorrowful innocence and a single tear slid down his cheek.

"Sargon Danaan died in the fire, officer. I saw it with my own eyes."

"Jesus," Markham was taken aback. "You've almost got me convinced."

"I'll back Arthur up to the hilt," Brandon said. "He was on his own when I encountered him. I'll not waver from his version and I'll make sure Tyres does the same."

"Then we'll stick to that story," the Deputy Chief said. "All of us. No interviews or comments to the press. We were just doing our job. Got that?"

His men nodded again.

"I was in charge," Markham pursed his lips. "So I'll personally take responsibility for not preventing Sargon Danaan's demise. High time I retired anyway."

He saluted his men, stiff and straight. They returned the gesture.

"Let us consider the matter closed."

Bailly and Brandon watched the performance in awe.

That was why the Deputy Chief was a legend.

38

Sargon pulled the rim of the helmet over his eyes and turned the collar of his uniform up. With his bulky frame and dirty face, he blended in perfectly. Brandon took Courage's arm and led her aside.

"With all that grime on your kisser, everyone believes you're an adult," he said. "I think Markham and Bailly may have their suspicions, but they won't give you away now. You're just an unidentified nurse who got caught up in the action."

"Thank you."

"I'll get you out of here as soon as there's an opportunity."

"Jefferson? Noakes?" Bailly pointed to the nearest men. "Take Arthur to the hospital."

"I will do it." Sargon stepped forwards. "It is only right that we finish this together."

He stumbled on the rough ground and fell. A few fire-fighters started towards him but Courage gestured them away.

"He's fine."

She helped the shattered boy up and both took the wheelchair handles. They began to push, struggling to manoeuvre Arthur over the marshy ground, turned into a near swamp by myriad hoses.

One fireman marched ahead of them, stopped and did an about-face. Another came and stood next to him.

Silently, the rest joined in, forming two lines on either side of the teenagers. They raised their axes in unison, creating an arch for the trio to pass under. As they reached each man, he removed his helmet and saluted.

"Oh wow," Arthur said quietly.

He reached back and took his friends' hands.

"This is indeed a fine send off," Sargon smiled to himself. "I do not need to go my funeral now."

"Wasn't keen on attending myself." Courage slyly elbowed him. "This is the only outfit I have left."

As they reached the cordon separating the main hospital from the emergency site, the fire-fighters fell in line behind them. A group of doctors and nurses were waiting.

"I fear this is goodbye." Sargon backed off and Bailly took over. "May we meet again someday. In something that isn't burning."

The firemen surrounded him until he became just another uniform in a sea of brown and yellow.

"So long, Arthur." Courage ruffled his sooty hair. "Keep it real, eh?"

"Always."

"I'll be off before I indulge in a public display of affection."

"No. Can't have that."

Arthur glanced back as Brandon led her away. He could tell from the way the girl's shoulders shook that she was crying.

Safely back inside the cordon, Brandon stopped to let his companion dry her tears.

"Go round the back of the building and head down the hill until you reach the street," he said. "Everyone will be concentrating on Arthur for the next few minutes."

"OK."

He looked guilty

"I'd come with you but…"

"But you'll be fending off reporters for the next few hours. Quite right, too."

"You should be sharing that glory." Brandon scratched his neck awkwardly. "Are you sure that…"

"I'm sure." Courage patted his cheek. "Look after yourself, hero."

She walked off and the fire-fighter ran back the way he had come.

Brandon was right. Nobody gave the girl a second glance. She was dressed the part, after all. A worn out nurse finally going home. Only she didn't have a home.

The storm was finally winding down and, at last, rain had begun to fall. Damp pavements glistened under misty coronas of yellow street lights, lighting the long, lonely road leading back to the city.

Courage shivered and rubbed at goose bumps rising on her arms.

The downpour was heavier now, washing the dirt from her face, making her look younger with each passing second.

As the girl started off again, she heard footsteps running behind her.

"I'll be all right, Brandon. I promise."

"Who's Brandon? The hunky guy that just left?"

Courage turned and gave a start.

"I'd like to talk." A large sister was waddling towards her, breathing heavily. "If you don't mind."

Her name tag read *Doreen Jones*.

"The emergency is over." Courage kept her face averted. "I'm not needed."

"None of the staff are allowed to leave until the firefighter's injuries have been seen to," Doreen wheezed. "But you've done plenty already, haven't you?"

Courage froze. An icy chill slid down her spine, one that had nothing to do with the temperature.

"What do you mean by that?" She tensed, ready to break into a sprint. Hopefully, she still had enough energy to outpace the woman.

But she wanted to know what the stranger meant more than she craved sanctuary.

"You've been inside the cordon all along," Doreen said. "I was watching from the top window of the new hospital. You could have escaped in the confusion at any time, but you stayed to help."

"What are you talking about?" The girl's eyes narrowed. "Why would I want to *escape*?"

"Because you're the runaway who prowled the corridors at night and used to sleep in the basement. Soon as I got close enough, I recognised you."

"Wait," Courage stammered. "You *knew* about me?"

"All the staff did. We left you alone because the old janitor, Grant Coull, asked us to." Doreen smiled gently. "Everyone loved that guy."

"But I was stealing things."

"That's why we locked our valuables away. We'd leave a bag lying around now and then, though, with a little money in it. Grant couldn't afford to support you on his crappy salary but he would have tried. He was like that."

"I… eh…." Courage was lost for words.

"Anyway, I just had a little chat with Arthur Lawson. Asked who made such a fine job of bandaging his wound. He looked flustered but he's quick with a fib, that kid. Said he didn't catch the name of the nurse, but she was a real credit to her profession. Then I spotted you slinking off."

"I don't bloody slink." Courage gave up pretending. "I'd just be in the way now. I'm not a real nurse, as you well know."

Doreen's hair was plastered to her scalp but she didn't seem to notice.

"Would you like to be?"

"*What?*"

"Would you like to be?" Doreen repeated. "I... eh... have a spare bedroom in my house. You could stay there while I scope out courses and stuff. Maybe pull a few strings."

"Why would you do that?"

"Good nurses show initiative. More than that, they care." Doreen approached slowly, palms up. "That's you, isn't it?"

"You don't know me."

"Grant Coull did, and he was a very perceptive man. Plus, I've been dealing with Arthur for a long time and he's never had a good word for anyone in the medical profession."

She gave a brief bark of laughter.

"You must have a terrific bedside manner. I bet he's not said anything that nice about me."

Courage rubbed tired eyes.

"I'd make a terrible tenant," she said hesitantly. "I'm a vegetarian, for a start."

"I'm offering to be your landlady, not a personal chef."

"I... eh... have real problems with authority."

"Ditto. I was moved to the Eyesore because I punched a snooty surgeon in the mouth."

Courage stifled a weary giggle.

"I won't take charity." She pulled a tattered plastic bag of cash from inside the uniform. "I can pay my way."

"Then what do you say?" The woman edged closer. "Will you accept my offer? Try to change the world for the better, even if it's just a little bit?"

"No offence," Courage tapped shredded fingers together. "But I don't *want* to be a nurse."

"You don't?" The woman looked puzzled. "I thought…"

"Rather become a doctor."

"Even better," Doreen beamed. "I get the feeling you'd achieve anything you set your mind to."

Behind them, the building gave a groan and began to topple. They turned and watched silently as it slowly collapsed, sending one last defiant spiral of fire into the night sky.

Courage reached out and took Doreen's hand.

39

Arthur sat looking at the open letter on his lap. His new room in the main hospital had a flat screen TV and large, clean windows that actually opened.

There was a tap on the door. The boy looked at his watch.

"There are only five minutes of visiting time left," he shouted. "If you're another reporter, go away. I told you I had nothing to say."

The door opened and a figure walked in. He wore a white tracksuit and an Avengers baseball cap, with the brim pulled as low as possible. Arthur goggled at him.

"Sargon?" A huge grin spread across his face. "Sargon! What are you doing here?"

"Shhhhhh." The boy put a finger to his lips. "I am in disguise, like Clark Kent."

"So you dressed as a juvenile delinquent? You'll have every security guard in the hospital following you."

"I am adept at eluding the flatfeet in this country, but I cannot stay long." Sargon sat on the bed and sniffed appreciatively. "These are much finer surroundings than you had before, I am glad to say."

He raised his arm.

"Now give me the highest of fives, for I am over the moon to greet you."

"Me too, buddy." Arthur slapped his palm.

"Did I hear mention of reporters?"

"They've been clamouring to pay for my story. I guess I'm a bit famous." Arthur wheeled over to the bedside table and poured them both a glass of water. "But I'm refusing to talk."

"Then you are between the horns of a Dalai Lama. The press will never give up until your beans are spilled."

"Taken care of," Arthur winked. "I told them I have post traumatic stress from watching you die and can't remember a thing after that."

"Ah, you are a sly one." Sargon furrowed his brow. "But you could sorely do with the cash. You said as much to me before."

"I got a job."

"Let me guess," his friend smirked. "You are the new janitor?"

"Deputy Chief Markham put a word in for me with Lothian Fire and Rescue Service." Arthur could hardly contain his glee. "When I turn sixteen, they're going to hire me as a consultant, advising on emergency evacuation procedures for disabled people. That guy is a legend."

"So I have heard several times now." Sargon sighed. "It did not stop him taking away my axe."

"The pay isn't much but that doesn't matter," Arthur enthused. "YouTube already has a dozen clips of my escape, filmed on mobile phones. I've entered them in the Parkour competition."

"Really?" His companion feigned innocence. "Is there a chance you will win?"

"Who's going to beat *that* stunt?" The boy kept a poker face. "I'll collect the £50,000 for sure."

"There *is* no competition, Arthur." Sargon raised one bushy eyebrow and tutted. "I checked."

"Ah." The boy looked ashamed. "Forgot you were the suspicious type."

"So why did you pull that stunt on the roof when we first met, my devious chum? It had nothing to do with money, I'll wager."

"You know damned well why."

"I wish to hear it from the horse's mouth. Courage and I both exposed ourselves to you, after all."

"Not really the best way to put it, as usual."

"Arthur," Sargon warned. "Do not be elusive."

"It's… difficult for me to say out loud."

"Try. You have survived worse."

"I wanted to feel truly alive one last time," Arthur said slowly. "Then I was going to let go."

"So the camera was to record your suicide?" Sargon nodded. "That is very up to date and down with the kids."

"No! The camera was to show you weren't in on it. I didn't want you getting into more trouble."

"Surely it would have smashed when you hit the ground?"

"As you keep reminding me, I'm rotten at making plans."

"You are incorrigible."

"Besides, I don't want to die anymore," the boy said. "I'm *not* useless. I may never walk again but there's plenty I *can* do."

"I am exceedingly thankful to hear it." Sargon squinted at the letter on his friend's lap. "So... What is contained in this missive you keep glancing at?"

"Aw, nothing important."

"As well as considerable charm and an exceptionally chiselled jaw, I have many other talents. One of them is being able to read writing that is upside down."

"Jeez." Arthur handed over the letter. "Nothing gets past you, does it?"

"I cannot believe you fell for that." Sargon scanned the page quickly while Arthur pretended to sulk.

"It is from a publishing company wishing to turn your adventure into a book."

"I know that. I've read it six times."

Sargon looked up in astonishment.

"They are offering you a preposterous amount of cash! You must accept."

"I'm not going to say I survived all on my own. I'd have died a dozen times if it weren't for you and Courage. I couldn't even give you any of the money without arousing suspicion."

"So what? I am a practical fellow, as I have repeated until your ears are black and blue. Courage and I can walk and you cannot. You need it all."

"It would come in handy," the boy admitted.

"Here is what you must do." Sargon jabbed a finger into Arthur's chest. "You will claim to have recovered your memory and invent a splendid tale of your der-ring-doos. You are a very accomplished fibber, as we both know."

"I prefer to call it a vivid imagination."

"Courage was never there," Sargon continued. "I died in a heroic manner at the beginning of your adventure. Make sure someone handsome plays me in the movie version. They cannot be short. Or ginger."

"To be honest, I'd say anything to get out of this place," Arthur said. "But that's simply not fair."

"Life is not fair. You, of all people, understand that. Now take that money and try not to spend it on loose women and bling. Courage and I can make our own way in the world. What else is there to do?"

They sat quietly for a few minutes.

"Will I see either of you again?" Arthur asked at last.

"I fear not. Should anyone find out I am alive or that Courage was with us, our house of cards will soon come tumbling down."

Sargon shook his head.

"Brandon, Bailly and vast Doreen will be getting the jackboot for hiding Courage's presence in Eden

Heights. She will be branded a thieving arsonist and never become a doctor. I shall be hunted down by immigration. My family will suffer. You will lose your new job and every word you say from then on will be suspected as a porkie-pie."

"But I'll be *living* a lie," Arthur objected. "That's going to feel a lot worse than telling one."

"You will get used to it." Sargon smiled sadly. "I did."

He got off the bed and looked in the mirror. For the first time in years, he did not hate what he saw.

"The three of us were forged in that fire and rose from the ashes. It is time to move on."

"Where will you go?"

"Now that I have been declared extinct, it may be safe for me to sneak back to my own country, for I am first rate at disguising myself, as you can plainly see. There are many who need help. I have certain... skills. I trust they may be finally put to good use."

"Like a superhero?"

"Indeed. Like a superhero."

He tapped the peak of his Avengers cap.

"For instance, I am going to pay a little visit to Courage's father." His eyes darkened and he gave a shark-like smile. "Dissuade him from looking for her further."

Arthur's eyes widened. For a second, he caught a brief glimpse of the person his companion used to be. The look was gone as quickly as it appeared.

"I am only joshing, of course," he said lightly.

But Arthur had the awful feeling he was deadly serious.

"So... this is goodbye, I fear." Sargon took his companion's hand and shook it warmly. "Though Courage has promised to write you."

Before the boy could reply, the door opened and a security guard barged in.

"Just checking that you were all right." The man looked at the intruder's dark skin with undisguised suspicion. "Visiting hours are over."

"I'm fine," Arthur said quickly. "This is... eh.... "

"Name's Bruce Banner, mate." Sargon switched to a perfect Scottish accent. "Stop givin me the evil eye and go get yirsel a doughnut."

He winked at Arthur.

"See ya, big man. Take care, eh?"

"Of course. You know I'm not the kind to take risks."

Sargon drained his water and swaggered out of the door.

"You're English is getting worse, by the way," Arthur called after him.

Sargon grinned and raised a middle finger as he vanished into the corridor. Once he was gone, the guard turned to Arthur.

"Sorry, but do you actually know that guy? He looks a bit dodgy."

"Bruce Banner? I only spent one day with him, to be perfectly honest."

Arthur used the remote to switch on the television. It was a news report announcing yet another crackdown on illegal immigrants.

"But, yes. He's my best friend."

"Now you know everything." Courage finished her tale. "I never saw your dad after that night. But I did become a nurse. Then a doctor. Finally, I moved here. Wanted to do some good."

"I don't know what to say." Duncan Lawson put away his notebook.

"Nothing, hopefully. It's not a tale you should print."

"Isn't it time to finally tell the world? You and Sargon deserve to be recognised for what you did."

"Arthur's book about the fire made him famous. Because of that, he went on to be a champion for the disabled and a human rights activist." Courage took off her glasses and tucked them in a pocket. "He was respected for his honesty and sense of justice, so I won't sully his name by contradicting the official version of events. This story was just for you. I don't want it repeated."

"You have my word," Duncan said. "I take it you know what happened to everyone else?"

273

"Arthur kept me up to date in his own letters. Markham Silver, Bailly Cousins and Doreen Jones retired after long careers." Her lips tightened. "Sally Hampton and Brandon Gollege died twenty years ago, fighting the Gardner's Crescent fire."

Courage looked lost for a moment.

"They were all heroes. Your dad included."

Duncan waited until she had composed herself.

"What about Sargon Danaan, Dr Banner?" he asked finally. "I notice you adopted his pseudonym. Was that out of respect?"

"Not quite," the woman brightened. "I have his last name because we're married."

The bodyguard strolled over and kissed the top of her head.

"Bruce Banner, at your service," he smiled. "I'm not much of a talker at work, as it does not fit with my hard boiled image. Courage, however, has become a far chattier person."

"I *wondered* how she knew every bit of the tale so well," Duncan stammered. "Why didn't you say who you were before?"

"I am a suspicious type, as Arthur was always fond of reminding me." The man gave an unexpected smile. "Unfortunately, violence is the talent I have most use for in this forbidding place. Though I also cook a mean Shawarma."

He suddenly grew serious.

"I am assuming, since you found my wife's letters to Arthur, that my old chum has also passed away. We had not heard from him in some time."

"He died of cancer two months ago," Duncan said. "I wasn't sure if Courage knew, so I thought it more appropriate to give the news in person."

"Indeed. Arthur would not have wanted to burden us with his woes. He was like that."

The man's face softened and, for a second, Duncan glimpsed an echo of the teenager who had been his father's friend.

Courage wiped a tear from her eye, reached out and took her partner's calloused hand.

"Our sincerest condolences on your loss, Duncan."

"Thank you. And I'm grateful you kept dad's secret." The reporter picked up his bag and prepared to leave. "Sorry to have taken up so much of your time."

"Hold your horses," Courage tisked. "We wouldn't ask Arthur's son all the way out here and have him leave empty handed."

"What do you mean?"

"You came here to write a piece about a boy who showed great courage when trapped in a burning building. One where you felt the whole truth hadn't been told."

Courage gave a wry smile.

"You can still do it."

"I don't understand. I just promised not to publish anything about my father."

"I'm not talking about Arthur." She pointed to the recorder.

"Turn that thing back on."

"Eh… OK." Duncan flipped the switch, mystified.

Courage glanced at her husband.

"You've been waiting a lifetime for this opportunity, honey."

"I most certainly have." Bruce Banner cleared his throat.

"Many years ago," he said. "A refugee column was ambushed near the town of Arbhanjar, not far from here."

He put down his gun.

"In it was a young boy called Sargon Danaan…"

End

A young asylum seeker is in a serious but stable condition after a 'frenzied attack' by a gang, which police are treating as a hate crime.

BBC News

A heroic son carried his disabled mother as he battled his way right from the top of the burning tower block all the way down the stairs to the bottom. His parents are from Afghanistan.

The Telegraph

The first victim of the horrific Grenfell fire has been named as Mohammed Alhajali – a Syrian refugee who came to Britain to seek a 'better life'.

The Independent

But that was another life, one he wants to forget. The airstrikes, the screams, the beheadings, are behind him now... but only if the authorities don't discover that he had trained and served as a Lion Cub for the caliphate.

BBC News

ABOUT THE AUTHOR

Jan-Andrew Henderson (J.A. Henderson) is the author of 40 children's, teenage, YA and adult fiction and non-fiction books. Published in the UK, USA, Canada, Australia and Europe, he has been shortlisted for fifteen literary awards and is the winner of the Doncaster Book Prize, the Aurealis Award and the Royal Mail Award.

www.janandrewhenderson.com